TRUE GRAY

TRUE GRAY

JAMES EARL

TRICKMULE SCRIPTS, TEXAS

To James A. Earl III

who bequeathed to me a lifelong love of history

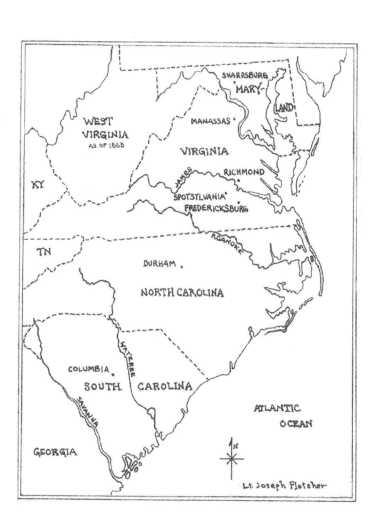

SHARPSBURG
MARY-
LAND
WEST
VIRGINIA
AS OF 1863
MANASSAS
VIRGINIA
KY
JAMES
RICHMOND
SPOTSYLVANIA
FREDERICKSBURG
ROANOKE
TN
DURHAM
NORTH CAROLINA
WATEREE
COLUMBIA
SOUTH CAROLINA
ATLANTIC
OCEAN
SAVANNAH
N
GEORGIA
Lt. Joseph Fletcher

TRUE GRAY

Sleep sweetly in your humble graves,
Sleep, martyrs of a fallen cause;
Though yet no marble column craves,
The pilgrim here to pause.

Henry Timrod, *Ode*

I was born of her womb;
I was nurtured at her breast;
and when my last hour shall come,
I pray God that I may be pillowed upon her bosom
and rocked to sleep within her tender and
encircling arms.

Edward Ward Carmack, *Pledge to the South*

CHAPTER ONE

(1850)

Beneath a green, mossy, cypress shed roof, Neptune, a thirty-year-old black servant, pulled a glowing red horseshoe from the forge with a set of tongs and hammered a few blows on the anvil, yellow sparks flying as the iron shimmered, its surface alive with dancing sparkles in response to the abrupt rearrangement of its molecules. A drop of sweat landed upon it and sizzled into vapor as Neptune turned the horseshoe over, examined it closely, then returned it to the forge. Young Mose, one of the house servants, barefoot in a homespun cotton shirt and calf length pants appeared behind him, silhouetted by the bright South Carolina sun.

"They wants you up at the big house."

TRUE GRAY

Mose watched curiously as Neptune tonged the horse shoe back out, laid it on the anvil, then removed his leather apron while streams of sweat rolled off his broad, dark, glistening forehead. Glancing back toward Mose, he smiled and winked, wiping his face with his shirt tail, then grabbed his stained straw hat and headed off, Mose following close behind him.

William Black's plantation house, a red brick monument to his sense of place in the world, lay solid and massive beneath huge sprawling chestnut trees on the western most edge of his four thousand acre plantation, five or so miles south of Columbia. Several multicolored cats having arisen from the porch, stretched and angled for attention as Neptune approached to find fifty something year old Americus, the head servant, in trim butler's garb and polished shoes, awaiting him by a hitched white mule, holding a packet of papers tied with a string.

"This here goes to the law office. They goin' to have some more papers for to bring back to Marse William. And this," handing him a slip of paper, "is for to get the Missus at the 'pothcarry."

Neptune examined the list, then placed it and the package of papers in the saddle bags, buckling the leather straps securely.

"Oh," said Americus, producing a note from his waist pocket. "Here's yo' pass. You don't want to get catched off'n the place without you got this. Now Marse William wants you back 'fore sundown."

Neptune mounted up.

"I'll be back. Sundown. Sure 'nough."

Neptune started the mule off at an easy walk down the long, cindered road that led straight out from the house, the steady crunch and scrape of hooves sounding off as if counting out the beats of a slow hymn. Slaves, on weathered ladders, pruning the tall elms that lined the road, waved to him as he passed below, while several women and children gathered the trimmings in wicker baskets. Reaching the gate, marked by two large red brick pillars, he reined the mule northward up Sutherford Road in the direction of town. Two negro boys busying themselves cleaning and polishing the rearing black iron stallions atop each column paused and watched, imagining what wonderous sights might await up the road.

TRUE GRAY

A slight breeze began to break the searing heat of late summer, billowy clouds temporarily blocking the sun as he passed fields of slaves hoeing beans, digging potatoes, picking okra and squash. Two old blacks mending a rail fence, one with a lame hand, stopped their work momentarily and nodded to him as he tipped his hat. Further on he became flanked by expansive cotton fields being worked by hundreds of sack wielding slaves, a mounted black overseer keeping watch. The overseer looked suspiciously at Neptune who feigned indifference. As he continued on, the fields at length gave way to a large stand of ash and poplar.

At a bend in the road he halted, pretending to adjust the mule's headstall, looking up and down the road carefully. A mocking bird harried a squirrel in the burr oaks above, knocking a couple of acorns to the ground. The squirrel having gained a safe distance, turned to fuss back. The breeze picked up in a brief gust, sending the rattle of fluttering leaves along the tunnel formed by the canopy of trees, then died to stillness. Neptune cast another careful glance in both directions, then with the driving sound of a claw hammer banjo in his head thumping out "Bee Gum Reel", urged the mule off the road, taking to the woods at a brisk trot. Reaching Peach Creek, he splashed in, then rode upstream for a piece before riding out on the opposite bank. Urging the mule back into a deliberate trot, he continued on through the woods.

Nathan Ledlow in shirt sleeves, sat at the dark walnut desk of his study, walls lined with bookshelves, a carefully inked survey of the Ledlow plantation neatly framed behind him, pouring over a ledger as Aunt Nettie refilled his coffee cup, her stout dark hands plying a lidded silver pitcher. Nathan smiled and nodded thanks as he took up a pen, dipped it into the inkwell, and carefully made an entry. Nettie left and closed the door quietly as the scratching noise of the pen on paper resumed. Completing the entry, he returned the pen to its holder and lifted the ledger, blowing lightly across the paper, when he heard a light tapping at the door. He returned the ledger to the desk and without looking, up consulted a stack of hand written receipts, untying the light blue silk ribbon holding them together.

"Yes? Come in."

Uncle Gabe, the Ledlow's head servant, balding, with a close silver beard, stepped in.

"Marse Nathan. Somebody here to see you, suh."

"Very well. Send them in."

Nathan lifted and studied one of the receipts closely while Uncle Gabe looked on uncomfortably, fingering a button on his vest.

"But Suh. It's one of Marse William's niggers."

Nathan looked up, pondering this for a moment.

"Very well. Send him in."

Uncle Gabe, puzzled, left the room.

Nathan turned in his oaken swivel chair and pulled the curtain aside slightly, giving him a view of the front drive. Toby, one of the servant boys, was standing holding a white mule, slicking the sweat off his withers with his hand. Gabe reopened the door and motioned to Neptune, who entered, hat in hand. Nathan nodded toward a chair as Neptune hesitated, self-consciously.

"I'd just a' soon stand suh... if'n it's okay."

"Certainly. What would be your name and what may I do for you?"

"Neptune Suh."

"Neptune..."

"Jus' Neptune suh," shifting his feet awkwardly. "I come for to ask you to buy my wife and children from Marse William."

"Oh?"

"They say you is kind suh. And treats your people fair."

"They?"

"The niggers 'round these parts. They all tell it."

Nathan gazed at Neptune who picked nervously at his hat.

"How many children and what ages?"

"I gots two suh. My boy, he ten, and my girl, she nine."

"And your wife?"

"Julia. 'Bout twenty-four, near as we can figure."

Nathan studied him closely.

"And what about you? Why would you consent to be separated from your family?"

Neptune looked down at his worn, home-made brogans.

"Please suh. Don't thinks bad o' me. Marse William... he ain't never lettin' go o' me on account I shoe his prize horses."

Nathan glanced down at his ledger.

"I really have all the negroes I can afford right now. Perhaps after the cotton is sold."

"But suh, Julia, she can do most anything you need. Cook, clean, mend. She works hard and honest. And my children, they mighty shy on account o' the way things is over there, but they minds real good. Please Marse Nathan. I begs o' you. Marse William so... I can stands it, but I can't bear to see my wife and children to suffer so."

Tears began to run down Neptune's dark dusty face.

"I'll think on it. That's all I can tell you right now. Is there anything else?"

Neptune wiped his eyes with his sleeve and looked up.

"Yes?"

"Suh. If'n Marse William was to find out I been to see you... he'll whip me sure."

Nathan ran a finger across his sealed lips.

"Thank you suh," turning to leave, then stopping at the door. "It's true what they been sayin'. I can tell it's true."

Neptune left, closing the door softly behind him. Nathan returned to his ledger for a moment, then stopped, turned and parted the curtain once more to see him heading out on the white mule. After a few strides, Neptune kicked the mule into a lope, the haunches of the mule digging in, kicking up dust as they receded into the distance down the road toward the main gate of the Ledlow plantation.

Americus, standing on the large, varnished, oaken planked porch of the Black's house, looked anxiously up the road. The door opened as William Black, forty-something, sinewy, pale, in fine high black leather boots and vest, stepped out, sleeves rolled up, wiping his face with a towel.

"He back yet?"

"Not yet, suh."

Americus avoided eye contact, continuing to scan the outer road to the north. William, his blood rising, worked his jaw muscles, unconsciously popping the towel on the thigh of his riding pants. His pale gray eyes narrowed in irritation as he glanced westward, the sun a giant red ball just about to clip the tops of the pitch pines on the horizon. Just then the sound of hoof beats at a lope were heard off in the distance, Americus craning his neck forward, intent on identifying the rider.

"There he is Marse William!" he said smiling nervously. "There he is... jus 'fore sunset!"

Neptune turned into the front gate, then slowed the blowing, sweating mule to a walk as he made his way up the elm lined road toward the house. William took one last look toward the west, then went back inside the house without a word.

CHAPTER TWO

Nathan's ten-year-old son Daniel launched a makeshift toy boat made of tree bark and twigs into the swirling eddies of Peach creek, nestled in a darkish wooded hollow. Following along the bank, he watched as the boat wound its way through the fast current of a bottle necked dog leg, past mossy rocks, nudging it back into the current with a stick when it hung up on a small shoal of smooth pink and gray pebbles. Skipping ahead around some boulders, he positioned himself to intercept the boat as it pitched over a miniature waterfall, tumbling up ended and pilotless. Daniel fished it from the water, turning it over in his hands to survey the damage, admiring its seaworthiness at being still intact. The sound of a wagon was heard then, passing unseen along the road above. Daniel took note, listening to the familiar sounds of his father's buckboard, the creaking of wood against wood, the jangling of trace chains, the clanking of iron wheel rims on the occasional stone in the hard-packed earthen road, the undulating sequence of two sets of hoof beats as the wagon receded into the distance, giving way once more to the babbling sounds of water and the

23

songs of the finches in the branches above. Seizing the stick, he scrambled back upstream to launch the bark boat once more.

Seated by the parlor window, Nathan's wife Sophia worked intently, her slender white hands plying a needle, embroidering a rectangle of cream colored muslin stretched in a steam bent wooden frame. It was a Bible verse she had chosen to frame and hang in the hallway outside the children's rooms, an admonishment regarding a recent tendency toward sibling discord. Completing the last stitch of the attribution, *Mark 3:24*, she removed it from the frame, smoothed it out and held it up to the light to appraise her work, when movement from outside the window caught her attention.

From his seat in a rocker on the porch, Uncle Gabe watched as Nathan approached in the buckboard, slowing the lathered matched bays to a walk. Beside Nathan rode an anxious looking negress, two small black children riding behind. Gabe arose and descended the porch steps as Toby, appearing from the side of the house, hurried forward to hold the horses. Nathan dropped the reins, set the brake, and stepped out as the children scrambled up beside their mother.

"Gabe, this is Julia and her little ones Washington and Bessie. See that they get situated please."

"Yes suh, Marse Nathan."

Nathan mounted the steps and entered the house, Gabe smiling at the newcomers, extending a kindly hand. Julia, nervously protective, held her arms tightly around her children, who returned wide eyed stares.

That afternoon toward the conclusion of dinner the Ledlows, seated around a long elegant chestnut table engaged in pleasant conversation. Nathan sat in his usual place at the head, while Sophia maintained the position opposite. Along one side were Daniel's twelve-year-old sister Ruth and eight-year-old sister Sarah, while Daniel sat on the other beside Nathan's brother Samuel, visiting from Columbia. Uncle Gabe topped off glasses of lemonade from a yellow stoneware pitcher, while Aunt Nettie, a long-time family servant, though no relation to Gabe, entered with a freshly baked pie. Setting it on the table, she promptly served up a generous slice on a plate and placed it before Samuel, who looked upon it in mock wonder.

"Sophie. I do believe you would have me fat!"

"Nonsense dear brother in law. We do however fret over you, for it is a well-known fact that a bachelor will routinely neglect adequate sustenance in his daily regimen."

"If by sustenance you mean luscious peach pie such as this, well I must then humbly plead guilty."

"Indeed," said Sophia. "I do hope you will consider staying the night with us, Samuel."

Aunt Nettie continued serving pie as Uncle Gabe commenced deftly taking up spent dishes and silver.

"Yes Sam. Please do," interjected Nathan. "We shall hunt quail in the morning if you like."

"Oh yes Uncle Samuel," said Daniel. "Please do stay over."

Samuel pretended to struggle with a decision.

"Well... will there be adequate sustenance?"

"Oh, better'n that Marse Samuel," said Nettie. "There'll be biscuits an' gravy!"

TRUE GRAY

Toby held four horses in the woods at the edge of an open field of larkspur and sage grass, the sun having newly cleared the line of jack pines looming high above, bathing the arena before them to the westward as if freshly lit for a stage performance. Nathan and Samuel, bearing fine side by side shotguns of English make, their figured walnut stocks and Damascus barrels gleaming, walked slowly, thirty feet apart, Daniel following a few paces behind. Two Shropshire spaniels patrolled eagerly ahead. Suddenly a covey of blue quail took to the air with a start, flapping and warbling in alarm. Samuel and Nathan, bringing their pieces to shoulder as one, took aim and fired, white plumes of smoke billowing forward, accompanied by the familiar pungent smell of sulfur and saltpeter. Three birds faltered in flight and fell to the ground as the spaniels sprang forward in a mad race to retrieve them.

"Good shot Sam! Two to my one!"

The dogs sniffed about in the brush, tails high, then ran back to Daniel eagerly dropping a bird each at his feet. Daniel stuffed them in his shoulder bag.

"Get the other one. Go Bose. Go Blue!"

The two dogs ran off in a frenzy, sniffing the weeds frantically for the other quail.

Later, Nathan and Samuel rode back toward the house with Daniel and Toby following, the spaniels racing ahead, reluctant to call it a day. Nathan motioned for Daniel to come up. Daniel nudged his mount to a trot and came along side.

"Next time out, you shall shoot."

Daniel smiled excitedly, looking at Samuel, who returned an approving nod.

"But you must remember all I have told you. A gun is a most valuable tool, but a danger if handled carelessly."

"Yes Papa."

Toward midday Toby, beside the cook house, was bent over a table strewn with quail, dressing them with a knife. A mishmash of feathers, wings and legs lay in a basket on the ground while Toby, rinsing off another light-colored breast in a bucket of water, laid it gently alongside the others on a large tinned pan. A cadre of cats circled around with great interest.

In the workshop Daniel, standing at a bench, wiped down one of the shotguns with care and placed it in the gun rack. He then turned his attention to the other one, removing the barrels, laying the stock gently on a cloth draped across the bench. Dipping a cotton patch in a mixture of goose grease and kerosene and fixing it into the end of the brass cleaning rod, Daniel commenced running it deliberately up and down the bore as he had been taught. Nathan appeared at the workshop door. Daniel, noticing, looked up.

"Daniel, I have someone I wish you to meet."

Nathan entered the workshop, herding Julia's reluctant son Washington gently by the shoulder. Daniel, cleaning rod in hand, looked at him, not comprehending.

"This is Washington. He is henceforth to be your body servant," then to Washington, "this is your new master, Daniel."

"What is a body servant, Papa?"

"A body servant is one who will always be there to help you with anything you need."

Daniel, puzzled, looked at Washington then at his father.

"But Papa. I don't need any help."

Nathan smiled, then dropped his hand from Washington's shoulder.

"You will."

TRUE GRAY

Nathan left, leaving Washington standing by the wall near the door. Daniel eyed him quizzically for a moment, then went back to cleaning the remaining shotgun, working the patch back and forth. He removed the rod, took off the blackened patch, then placed a clean one on the rod and continued swabbing the second bore. He glanced over his shoulder to see Washington standing in the same place as before, watching. At length, satisfied with the barrels, he pricked the nipples clean, blowing through them to insure they were clear, then reassembled the gun, wiping it down with a lightly oiled cloth. Washington continued to look on as Daniel placed the gun in the rack, then headed out the door.

Daniel made his way across the yard toward the front porch, Washington following about ten paces behind. Climbing the steps, he took a seat on the porch swing and set it in motion, watching as Washington sat shyly on the first step. Stretching lengthwise on his back Daniel closed his eyes, drifting off into a wonderous day dream of his first taking of a quail, the glory of the hunt, the excited pant of the Shropshires, the pride in his father's face. He dozed for a while amid the sounds of buzzing flies, an occasional shift of breeze high above in the walnut trees, the distant musical strain of black voices at work in a nearby bean field. A horse whinnied from the stables, then snorted and shook. Aunt Nettie's jovial laughter rang from the kitchen, followed by the smell of something baking which wafted gently on the summer air, through the house and across the front porch. At this Daniel awoke, sat up in the porch swing and rubbed his eyes. Washington remained, still sitting on the steps, watching him. Daniel stood up, stretched, then entered the house, following his nose.

In the kitchen, he found Aunt Nettie in her wide ample indigo dress, hair back in a gingham scarf, mixing vigorously a large yellow earthenware bowl of cornbread stuffing to go with the quail. Seeing Daniel out of the corner of her eye she smiled but continued to stir.

"Nettie, I'm going down to the creek for a while."

Nettie stopped and wiped her large capable hands on her apron.

"Okay honey. I'll tell your folks if'n they ask. You bes' be back by supper though. The quail is gwine to be my crownin' achievement."

Aunt Nettie opened a brown pottery crock and pulled out a couple of corn dodgers, wrapping them in a cloth and handing them to Daniel.

"'Case you get hungry 'fore then." She placed her hand lovingly on his cheek. "Now don't you go gettin' in no mischief."

"I won't Nettie," said Daniel, taking the cloth bundle and hurrying out.

Daniel came out of the door, skipped down the porch steps past Washington and headed for the woods. Washington, taken off guard jumped up and followed. Reaching the split rail fence at the edge of the woods, Daniel crouched and stepped through. Seeing Washington in pursuit, he struck a trot into the dark dense stand of poplars and yellow birch trees, hopping over fallen logs, skirting tree trunks, ducking under low limbs, wrens skittering before him from branch to branch. Glancing back and seeing Washington about fifty feet behind him, he picked up the pace as if a fox pursued by hounds. Reaching the creek bank beneath dark towering cypress trees, he stopped, trying to still his breath, listening for footsteps. With nothing to be heard but the babbling of the water spilling over the small fall into the deep clear pool, he placed his cloth bundle on a rock and doffing his hat and clothes haphazardly, dove with a gratifying splash into the cool depths of Robber's Hole.

Underwater, Daniel swam open eyed past perch and minnows where a cave like assemblage of cypress roots decorated the walls of the watery underworld. Bubbles drifted from his nose, his reddish blonde hair waving, as he stroked by a goodly sized mud turtle which leisurely paddled its way to a safe haven beneath the roots. Undulating light danced upon the silted floor laden with colored stones as he turned upward and broke to the surface, treading water, slicking his hair back and clearing his face. Washington stood at the shore, watching in alarm.

Daniel swam leisurely over toward the familiar shallow rock and took a seat in the water. Washington, somewhat relieved, sat down on the bank by Daniel's clothes.

"How come they call you Washington?"

"I don't know. That's the name they give me. Folks calls me Wash."

"Where you from?"

"The black place."

"The black place? Where is that?"

Wash looked up through the mossy cypress branches, checking the sun, then pointed roughly eastward. Daniel pondered this for a moment.

"Mister Black's Plantation?"

Wash nodded as Daniel squirted water up into the air with his fists.

"Want to swim?"

"No suh. I don't swim."

"Why? Don't you know how?"

"No suh."

"Well that's too bad. There's nothing better. You really should learn. Watch."

Daniel pitched off backwards into the hole, Wash jumping to his feet in wonder, straining to see Daniel's ivory white body, breast stroking easily ten feet below in the crystal depths. After an anxious moment Daniel breached like a whale, laughing.

"See? Nothing to it."

He continued to swim across the hole and back, frolicking in the water like an otter, rolling on his back and spouting water from his mouth, causing Wash to smile. Finding his seat on the rock once more, he reached for the cloth bundle and unwrapped it.

"Look what Nettie made. Corn dodgers. She makes the best in the whole blamed county."

He lifted one up lightly, showing off the thing in all its crusted, brownish yellow beauty, and began munching away. He extended the other to Wash.

"Want one?"

Wash looked at it, tempted.

"No suh."

"Why not? They're awful good. Honest. Aren't you hungry?"

"I ain't 'sposed to. If'n they was to find out..."

"Here Wash. Eat it. It's okay."

"You won't tell?"

Daniel made Nathan's gesture, running a finger over his sealed lips. Wash reluctantly accepted the dodger taking a big bite, relishing the taste of spiced cornbread and bacon grease as they sat silently eating, listening to the water, sharing in the combined blessings of Aunt Nettie's cooking and the glory of a southern summer. Finishing his, Daniel took several more turns down into the waters, exploring the bottom for treasures, playfully pursuing the fish as Wash anxiously awaited each of his returns to the surface. At length Daniel climbed out and slicked water off his legs and arms, shaking his wet head like a puppy shedding water. Going to dress, he found his clothes neatly folded in a pile beneath his felt hat.

With the sun lower in the sky, Aunt Nettie stepped out onto the porch, shielding her eyes with her hands, looking in the direction of the creek to find Daniel approaching with Wash following.

"There you is Marse Dan'l. And none too soon. Supper is just 'bout ready. You best go scrub them paws."

Nettie held the door as Daniel walked up the porch steps past her and entered. Wash stopped at the steps, unsure of what to do. Nettie gave him a stern look, then went in and closed the door. Julia appeared from the direction of the servant's cook house.

"Wash honey. You come on over here with us. We gonna eat soon enough."

CHAPTER THREE

Two mounted riders, eleven-year-old Bobbie Hawkins and nine-year-old Joe Fletcher, made their way leisurely through the woods, picking a path through the trees. A rooting armadillo sniffed the air, then scurried off noisily through the leaves, the ponies shying briefly. A squirrel eyed them, edging its way quietly around the opposite side of a large walnut tree. Reaching a thicket, they dismounted and tethered their ponies to saplings.

At Robber's Hole, Daniel, waist deep in the shallows, waited on Wash standing naked and hesitant on the bank.

"Is there snakes in there Marse Dan'l?"

"I've never seen a snake in here Wash. Honest Injun. There's fish and turtles and such, but they're more afraid of us than we are of them."

Wash slowly eased into the water, testing the rocky bottom with his feet, making his way toward Daniel.

"All you have to do is move your arms like this," said Daniel, demonstrating, throwing each arm forward in succession, pulling back through the water with his palms flat.

Wash began to mimic his movement.

37

"Then just kick your legs any old way you like. I do like this."

Daniel held onto a cypress root and flutter kicked his legs out behind him, churning up the water like a paddle wheeled steamer.

"Or kick like a frog does. It doesn't matter."

Wash grabbed hold of the root and began trying to kick his legs, holding his head high out of the water.

"Lay flatter Wash. You gotta stretch out more, like a fish."

Something caught Wash's eye and he stopped suddenly. Bobbie and Joe were standing on the opposite bank, staring.

"I was thinking you boys might be coming over. Going for a swim?" asked Daniel.

Bobbie and Joe were transfixed.

"Come on. The water's fine."

Bobbie looked at Wash, then Joe, then back toward Daniel.

"We don't swim with niggers."

Wash looked fearfully to Daniel.

"Oh... this is Washington. He's not a nigger. He's my body servant. I'm teaching him to swim."

Bobbie exchanged another look with Joe.

"He looks like a nigger to us," said Bobbie.

They turned to leave.

"Well, if you're afraid to get in, I guess we got it all to ourselves.

Bobbie stopped short.

"We ain't afraid of nothin'."

"Well, did you come to swim or not?" said Daniel.

Later, the ponies grazed placidly on their tethers, bending the saplings to nibble fresh grass. At Robber's Hole, Bobbie, naked, edged his way out along an overhanging cypress branch ten feet above the water. Daniel and Wash were crouched neck deep in the water, Wash working on his arm stroke. Joe having just popped up from below treaded water and looked up, then paddled toward Daniel and Wash to get out of the way. Reaching his desired spot, Bobbie gingerly got his feet beneath him and raised to a standing position, arms spread out for balance.

"I'm a redcoat sniper. Shoot me!"

Daniel took mock aim with an imaginary rifle.

"Bang!"

Bobbie grabbed his chest dramatically, made a grimace, heaved a sigh, then fell backwards into the water with a splash.

"Good shot Dan'l," said Joe.

Wash laughed. Popping to the surface, Bobbie breast stroked triumphantly toward the others.

"You sure are a good die-er," said Joe.

"My father has a real Mississippi rifle. He's gonna let me shoot it soon as I turn twelve," Bobbie said.

"My daddy has a whole cabinet full of guns," replied Joe, not to be outdone.

Daniel, thinking of his upcoming quail hunt, remained silent. Bobbie looked toward Wash and then at Daniel.

"How come you have a body servant?"

"To help me with anything I might need."

"Like what?"

"I don't know. I haven't needed him to do anything yet."

"Well what good is he if he don't do nothin'?" piped up Joe.

"Yeah Daniel," said Bobbie. "Make him do something. We want to see."

Wash looked at Daniel questioningly, while Daniel thought for a moment.

"Okay. Wash, splash him!"

Wash shoved water with both hands, hitting Bobbie full in the face, leaving him coughing and blinking, dumfounded. Joe, tickled, began to laugh. Bobbie turned and splashed Joe, catching him open mouthed as an all-out splash fight erupted, all four boys churning up water with glee. Back up the embankment, beside the thicket, the ponies stopped their munching momentarily to lift their heads, fresh green grass hanging from their muzzles, ears perked toward the distant sounds of the battle of Peach Creek.

CHAPTER FOUR

Standing in the foyer of the Ledlow house, Sophia straightened Daniel's string tie as Aunt Nettie dusted lint off the shoulders and back of his jacket. Daniel, uncomfortable, trussed up in his go-to-town clothes with a tied bundle of books under his arm, bore being fussed with bravely.

"There now Master Ledlow. This shan't be as bad as all that. Mr. Durham comes highly recommended as one of Columbia's finest educators," said Sophia, brushing Daniel's rebellious hair behind his ears tenderly with her fingers. "And you won't be by yourself this session."

"Tha's right Marse Dan'l. This time you'll be schoolin' with yo' friends," interjected Nettie.

"But Mama, wouldn't it be better for me to stay and help Papa?"

"Oh, I'm sure your father would appreciate that mightily, but a young southern gentleman must not only be brave and strong, he must be learned as well."

She kissed him tenderly on the cheek, as Nettie placed his best felt hat on his head, and turned to open the door. Resigned to his grim fate, he went out, Sophia and Nettie exchanging sympathetic looks.

Out front Wash stood waiting, holding Daniel's gray pony. Daniel walked down the steps, toward the pony, which flicked its tail at a fly and stepped to the side a bit. Daniel handed the books to Wash, then mounted taking the reins, as Wash tied the bundle of books to brass rings behind the smooth, brown, freshly soaped plantation saddle.

"I 'spect I best go along with you, Marse Dan'l."

"No Wash. That won't do. I'll be doing nothing but sitting in a stuffy school all day. You stay here and see if Toby needs help with anything. I'll be back. Late afternoon."

Daniel headed off at a walk, like a convict bound for the gallows. Wash stood and watched as he rode out to the gate, then disappeared down the road.

That afternoon Daniel sat at a long table in a study in the Fletcher House with five other boys, listening to a pointer wielding Horatio Durham Esq. in a worn black woolen waist coat and stiff white collar, lecture. Bobbie and Joe exchanged looks of despair with Daniel, mutual in the grave acceptance of this miserable turn of events.

"...for we must ever remember, a curious mind is a sound mind. Education my boys, is the fountain from which all greatness springeth."

Mr. Durham motioned with his slim, brass tipped pointer to three printed portraits in gold leaf frames on the wall, one each of Franklin, Jefferson and Washington. As Daniel studied the grim, sober countenance of Washington, he suddenly detected movement through the partially opened window behind Mr. Durham. It was Wash, feeding Daniel's pony handfuls of picked grass.

"And so boys, by Wednesday this, you shall have read through chapter two of McGuffey's. In addition, I will expect all of you to have your times tables through six memorized. Our class is hereby adjourned."

As the boys scrambled to escape, Daniel retied his books, retrieved his hat from the rack and, nodding respectfully toward the stern schoolmaster, headed off. Outside, Wash was combing the pony's mane with his fingers.

"Wash, what are you doing here?"

"Making sure your pony's fit for to ride home, Marse Dan'l."

"I thought you were going to help Toby."

"I did. He set me to oiling up all the wagon harness, but I done finished," said Wash smiling, holding the bridle for Daniel to mount.

The afternoon was pleasant, made more so by having just survived his first day of captivity, as riding, Daniel made his way along the winding shadowy dirt path toward home. His pony walked easily, crunching dry leaves beneath his hooves as Wash walked along behind.

"I figured out today who you're named for, Wash."

"Who, Marse Dan'l?"

"George Washington."

"Who's that?"

"Who's that? Why he's the father of our country."

"My father be Neptune."

"No Wash. This is different. George Washington is the father of America. All of us."

"Where's he live then?"

"He's not alive anymore. He's in heaven."

Wash looked upward, pondering this for a moment, then side stepped a fresh pile of dung dropping from the gray.

"Was he good, Marse Dan'l?"

"Oh, he was a great man."

"Reckon they called him Wash?"

They continued on, crossing the shallow tributary of Peach creek that delineated the northern boundary of the Ledlow plantation, the pony stopping to take a drink, while Wash picked his way barefooted across a row of dry rocks. The pony, having gotten his fill, lifted his drizzling muzzle as Daniel reined him out of the stream and up the embankment southward through the Ledlow's expansive timber lot of balsam fir, beech and longleaf pine.

"So after reading and spelling, we had a lesson in arithmetic and then history. History isn't half bad though, because we get to learn about famous battles and such."

"What's rid-a-tick?"

"Arithmetic. It's learning about numbers. How to add and subtract... and multiply. You've got to know all about it or you won't be able to keep track of anything, like how many bales of cotton you have to sell, or how many calves you're going to have come springtime, or how much a negro is worth. Wash stopped to quickly pull a sticker from his foot, then hurried to catch up.

TRUE GRAY

"You really ought to know arithmetic too Wash, if you're going to be my body servant."

"How'm I gonna learn it, Marse Dan'l?"

"I'll teach you, same as Mr. Durham teaches me."

Nathan sat in his shirtsleeves in his study, making out a writ of sale for hay. It had been a marginal cutting, but the stacks were clean of spear grass, and drying nicely. One hundred and seventy-two stacks, averaging about one hundred and twenty-five cubic yards a piece. The Columbia Guard had taken all he could spare, storing up against the coming winter. There would be possibly one more cutting before the first frost, but still with the possibility of a shortage looming, timothy in the field should sell for about ten cents a yard one would think... perhaps a bit more. Nathan's thoughts were distracted by the sound of a voice outside, nearing.

"Two time two is four. Two time three is six," Wash recited, thinking. "Two time four is... ten."

"Eight," corrected Daniel.

"Eight. Two time five is..."

"Ten," said Daniel. "That's the one that's ten."

TRUE GRAY

Nathan glanced out the side window in time to see Wash riding behind Daniel on the gray as they made their way around the end of the house toward the stables. With raised eyebrow, he watched in amusement as they clopped along around the corner and out of sight, Wash holding on to Daniel's waist, his bare feet dangling freely. Shaking his head with a vague smile, Nathan returned to his work.

TRUE GRAY

CHAPTER FIVE

Robber's Hole was near silent, save the babbling of the cool clear water of the small fall spilling into the pool, the barely audible sound of the light air shifting direction in the wispy branches high above, the occasional song of a mocking bird mocking its neighbors. Daniel, near the spillway, worked a long slender cane pole, fine linen line running through a wire loop at the end, adjusting the length of excess line with his free hand, then clamping steady with the other when satisfied. Wash, doing likewise, fished near the outlet.

"How many you got there, Wash?"

"I got's three."

"I've got two so far. How many does that make?"

Wash considered for a moment.

"Five," pulling his line in and resetting his bait in a different spot. "Seem like they quittin' on these grasshoppers though. They ain't bitin' so good now."

"Aren't."

"What, Marse Dan'l?"

"Aren't. They *aren't* biting. Mr. Durham gets plumb mad if we say ain't. Even if it's on accident."

Wash hauled in his line, the impaled yellow green grasshopper torso still attached.

"Well, let's see if we can find us some grubs," said Daniel.

Up in the woods Daniel and Wash located a fallen rotted chestnut log and, shouldering in together, rolled it back, exposing the dark moist humus beneath. Several shiny speckled salamanders and a large orange legged centipede moved off quickly to greener pastures as the boys dropped to their knees and began digging eagerly through the rich dank earth with sticks.

"Here we is," said Wash, sifting a handful of dirt to expose several plump amber colored larvae, then dumping them into his upturned straw hat.

Daniel, working his stick, lifted two more and tossed them in.

"We gonna catch 'em now sure... a whole mess of fish," added Wash.

As they continued to harvest grubs, Daniel suddenly stopped, lifting something in his hand, rubbing away the dirt with his fingers.

"Hey. Look at this."

Wash leaned over to see.

"What's that?"

"Can't tell exactly."

Wash followed Daniel to the water's edge as he crouched to rinse clean his new find, then raised it from the water.

"It's a button... from a uniform."

Daniel stood up and maneuvered it into a patch of clear light filtering through the trees, rotating it slowly in his fingers.

"Look Wash. Look here," pointing. "See that part that looks like a tree?"

Wash looked closely trying to make it out. Daniel gave the button another scrub on his pants leg, then held it back up as they stood shoulder to shoulder examining it, modeled in browns, greens, and brassy tones, bits of white mineral incrusted in the recesses, a slight dent on one edge.

"That's a palmetto. It's on the South Carolina flag."

Wash gazed upon it in wonder as if it were a Spanish doubloon.

Toward afternoon, Daniel and Wash made their way back home, their poles over their shoulders like marching soldiers, each bearing a good-sized string of fish.

"Reckon I could get me a button like the one you got, Marse Dan'l?"

"I don't know Wash. It was a mighty lucky find."

"Maybe if'n I was to go back a diggin' 'round in the grubby-worm dirt."

Daniel shrugged, doubtfully, as they marched on for a spell, the silvery fish swaying and gleaming in the sun like treasures in their own right.

"We sure came up fine on the fishin' though," said Daniel proudly. "Ain't Gabe and Toby goin' to be jealous?"

"Aren't, Marse Dan'l."

Daniel gave him a puzzled look as they continued on.

CHAPTER SIX

The sun rose golden and glorious across the front of the Ledlow house, illuminating the glowing, white fluted columns, the slatted shutters bright against the darkish red brick facade, the silvery gray sheen of the cypress shingled porch roof. Toby stood by the wagon with a step stool, helping up Sophia, Daniel, Ruth and Sarah dressed in their Sunday finest. Nathan climbed in lastly as Toby stowed the step stool securely, then scrambled up to take the reins of the four-horse team. Uncle Gabe stood on the porch watching with a grin.

"See you this afternoon, Gabe," said Nathan.

"Sho' 'nough, Marse Nathan. The Lord be with you fine folks this day."

"And you."

Nathan nodded to Toby, who released the brake lever and tossed the reins, urging the team forward. Gabe waved to the children from the porch as they headed out the gate, then broke into an easy trot. A bumpy hour's ride brought them to Stoney Shoal Baptist Church, snuggled firmly and proudly, freshly whitewashed, in a clearing surrounded by an old growth stand of hickory and oak. Slowing the team to a walk, Toby drove the wagon up to the front, set the brake, then hopped out to retrieve the stepstool while fellows of the congregation waved and offered words of welcome. Toby lent a hand to Sophia and the girls, as the Ledlows made their way up the wooden steps of the church to join groups of people from all around, gathered near the front door, shaking hands and visiting pleasantly.

At the Ledlow plantation fifty or so negroes crowded into a low roofed, roughhewn, log structure, while others found seats on the board and post benches outside, under broad eaves, near rows of unglazed window openings.

The dark polished pews of Stoney Shoal Church had filled with eager, talkative practitioners of the faith. Sophia untied her bonnet and placed it carefully in her lap, as Daniel and his sisters dutifully took seats beside her. Nathan, hat in hand, exchanged a few pleasant words about the weather with an acquaintance in the pew ahead of them. A hush suddenly fell over the crowd as Reverend Stephen Coburn stepped up to the lectern.

The little log chapel was alive with talk as negroes, crowded on the flat board benches within, fussed with their children and visited gayly. Few women were without an infant or two on their laps, while eager faces peered through the window openings on the sides, the board shudders hinged above with leather, propped up by peeled saplings. Uncle Gabe, dressed in his best butler's coat, made his way to the front near a post driven into the dirt floor with a hand worn board nailed atop and, without a word, began clapping his hands slowly, rhythmically.

"Welcome my friends. Welcome to the house of the Lord," said Reverend Coburn, raising his hands, palms upward. "Let us sing."

Nothing was heard but the shuffling of leather soles on the waxed oaken floor and the rustling of dress fabric as the congregation gained its feet, hymnals in hand.

The hand clapping in the log chapel began to pick up in intensity as the crowd arose, the methodic beat spreading to those outside who followed suit, standing and clapping, shoulders starting to dip, heads beginning to bob. Wash tugged at Julia's sleeve.

"Mama."

"You ain't takin' sick again now is you?" she said, feeling his lower leg. "You still got your healin' hand?" She lifted up his frayed pant leg to reveal the herbal bundle tied with torn strips of indigo cloth above his ankle.

"Yeh mama... but I got's to pee."

"Lord child. Why didn't you go before?"

Wash shrugged.

"Well go then... but hurry or you're liable to miss somethin'."

The Stoney Shoal congregation rang out in eager, sober, song.

Rock of ages, cleft to me,
Let me hide myself in thee.
Let the water and the blood,
From the riven side which flowed...

Uncle Gabe, continuing to clap, sounded forth with full resonant voice, the congregation echoing in answer to each word, resounding in a rich symphony of natural tones, undertones, harmonics, harmonies.

We are... we are,
Climbing... climbing,
Jacob's... Jacob's,
Ladder... ladder,

With the sounds of "Jacob's Ladder" ringing in the distance, Wash stepped out of the outhouse, hurriedly buttoning his pants. A man's voice was suddenly heard, quiet and low.

"Wash!"

Wash looked innocently toward the direction of the voice at the edge of the woods. It was Neptune, standing, grinning nervously in the shadows. Wash ran to him, still fumbling with the last button.

"Paw-Paw!"

"Shhh now young'n... you'll be getting' the whole country up," said Neptune kneeling to give him a hug. "They treatin' you good over there? Getting' plenty to eat?"

"Yeh, Paw-Paw."

"How's your mama and sister?"

"They's good."

"I know'd thing's would be better."

Wash touched Neptune's scruffy short beard.

"Why don't you come live with us?"

"Cain't right now little'n... but I'll come see you much as I can." Neptune held Wash's head gently with his large calloused hands and looked him squarely in the eye.

"Now you don't tell nobody I was here Wash, exceptin' your mama. You understand?"

Wash made the sealed lips finger sign.

Uncle Gabe began moving around the room giving emphasis to the words with his hands, cueing and encouraging the congregation to ever heightening emotion.

Rise... rise,

Shine... shine,

Give God the... give God the,

Wash ran to Julia's side and joined in on the singing.

Glory... glory.

Wash tugged on Julia's sleeve. As she leaned toward him he whispered in her ear.

Rise... rise,

Shine... shine,

Gabe passing down the aisle cocked his ear, taking note of Wash's precociously strong voice.

Give God the... give God the,

Glory... glory,

Julia sang with eyes beginning to well up. As Uncle Gabe regained the front of the chapel, turning to the crowd with outstretched palms, the congregation joined him in unison, full throated and joyous.

Soldiers of the cross.

CHAPTER SEVEN

The woods to the east of the Ledlow house were awash in the first signs of fall, the broad leaves of the maple trees just beginning to show color at their bases, an amber shift predisposed to the brilliant reds and at length dark maroons they would become before letting loose and drifting down resolutely to the ground, sacrificial lambs to the inevitable cycle of the seasons. Wash and Daniel knelt together alongside a snared rabbit, it having succumbed sometime in the night to the stress of entanglement. Wash gently loosened the twine from its neck, then lifted it by its tufted hind feet, the mottled gray fur soft as a cloud.

"He's a fat 'un Marse Dan'l," said Wash, turning it, admiring it in the forest light. "Jus' look at that belly."

Daniel carefully reset the snare over the rabbit trail, propping the string with a notched stick, then gently scattering crushed leaves and twigs over the trail to disguise the set.

"What'd you catch?" sounded a voice approaching through the woods from the south.

It was Bobbie, thumbs hooked in his britches, with Joe following close behind.

60

"Three rabbits," said Daniel, putting the finishing touches on the snare. Wash showed off the fat buck proudly before stuffing it in the pillow ticking game bag.

"That ain't nothin'. I got a fox last fall."

"My brother Ben...why he caught a bobcat once... and it was still alive and a snarlin'. He had to thump it with a stick," added Joe, acting out the thumping motion dramatically.

Daniel rose and brushed the leaves and sticks from his pants.

"Well you can't eat a fox or a bobcat far as I know. I'd just as soon have a rabbit."

"Rabbit is okay," replied Bobbie, winking at Joe. "But I've never had nothin' beats a lark for eatin. Say, Wash... you ever been a larkin'?"

"No suh."

"Well it's a bountiful heap of fun, and it's just about season for 'em. Ain't it Daniel?"

Wash looked to Daniel quizzically, who taken off guard, returned a reluctant smile.

"How we catches 'em?" asked Wash.

Bobbie, picking up a stick, knelt down and, with great authority, began to lay out the plan in the leaves, the others looking on.

"Best way is for us to fan out in a big wide circle. All but one of us that is. One of us has got to stay put with a sack or something. Then, when we drive the larks in real slow like, the feller with the sack, why he just scoops 'em up pretty as you please and stuffs 'em in."

"Who gonna be the one what does that?" asked Wash.

Bobbie stood up, hitching his britches, seemingly pondering the question with great circumspection.

"Well, seems to me Wash ought to get to do it, seein' as how he ain't never been a larkin' before."

"Yeh. Wash," said Joe.

Wash looked to Daniel who responded with a half-hearted shrug.

The promising light of morning gave way to a peculiar reddish glow, seeming to emit from nowhere and everywhere, shifting familiar colors to something other, muting tops of foliage, enlivening undergrowth. Daniel removed the rabbits from their game bag, bound the hindlegs together with a length of the snare twine and, slinging them over his shoulder, handed Wash the bag.

"Now, we'll have to go real slow and cautious like or the larks are liable to spook and bolt clean through us and get away," said Bobbie with a learned air. "You're gonna have to be real quiet and stay put till we bring 'em in. Okay Wash?"

Wash nodded eagerly.

"Alright then. We'll head out together this way," pointing over his shoulder with his thumb, "then fan out in three directions and start to working our way back. Agreed?"

"Agreed," replied Joe.

Bobbie and Joe looked at Daniel.

"Okay," replied Daniel.

The boys headed out single file with Daniel in the rear. Wash watched them as they wound their way off through the trees.

"Is they big Marse Dan'l?"

"No, Wash... they ain't big," called Daniel from a distance.

"But tasty," added Joe.

A hundred yards away Bobbie, Joe and Daniel stopped in a clearing.

"Boy, I'd give anything to see his face when he finally figures it out," whispered Bobby.

Joe chuckled as they parted ways, he and Bobbie heading westward, while Daniel stood in the silence gazing upward through the top branches of the trees, the reddish glow having taken a sudden turn to the dark, the air dead still.

Back in the woods, Wash knelt quietly, holding his pillow ticking game bag at the ready as the first blast of cool air brushed against his face, rippling the brim of his straw hat, the sky turning abruptly black and ominous.

Daniel, having made it back home, sat on the porch swing rocking back and forth gently with an occasional absent-minded push of his foot, reading his lesson, waiting for Wash to return, when a flash of light illuminated the page followed by a sharp clap of thunder. He folded the book and stepped to the porch rail, peering into the threatening sky.

In the woods, Wash, afraid, crouched at the base of a pine tree as the rain began to splatter down through the boughs, holding the bag over his head for protection. A bolt of lightning hit close by, shaking the ground, leaving an otherworldly scent of fresh split bark and boiled resin wafting in the gathering wind.

From the direction of the servant's quarters, Julia ran through the first sheets of rain toward the back of the main house, holding a straw hat on her head with one hand, her skirts gathered in the other while Daniel, from the porch, strained to see through the building torrent. After a few moments Nathan stepped out.

"Wash is missing Daniel. Do you know anything about this?"

"We were just having fun with him Papa. We took him a larkin'."

Nathan, jaw set, stiffening in controlled anger, held his hand out for Daniel's book.

"You had best go find him then."

"But Papa... it's a stormin'."

A flash of lightening lit up Nathan's face stern as stone, the wind whipping his flaxen hair back, his piercing gray eyes fixed on his son.

"He's your body servant Master Ledlow. Go!"

A crack of thunder sounded like a cannon shot as Nathan pointed into the tempest, sending Daniel down the steps and trotting off into the deluge. Sophia, unnoticed, having witnessed all, stepped out onto the porch and squeezed Nathan's arm, as the wind took a turn, driving rain across the porch, wetting them both. Nettie appeared just inside the screen door.

"He back Marse Nathan. Wet an' scar'd, but okay."

"Oh Nate," cried Sophia. "We must call Daniel off!"

"No Soph. He has to learn."

He placed his arm around her as, together, they watched the storm gather in strength and ferocity.

CHAPTER EIGHT

It was early as Aunt Nettie entered Daniel's room and placed a tray with a cup of warm broth on the bedside table. Parting the curtains, she opened the window to the rising sun and the clean fresh air of a post storm morning. Daniel was lying quietly, already awake, as Nettie turned from the window.

"Why Marse Dan'l, you's alive. Mercy be and praise the Lord. It's a wonder you both didn't catch your death. Looked like two drowned rats you did. Yes suh... a little white 'un an' a little black 'un." She picked up the cup of broth and lifted it to his lips. "Here now honey. You drink this up. It'll help to drive off the blue shivers."

Ruth, in a house dress and slippers, stepped into the room.

"Daniel. Papa wants to see you as soon as you're up. He's in his office."

Nathan sat at his desk with a porcelain cup of steaming black coffee in a saucer close at hand, reading the *Columbia Tribune*. He took a sip of the coffee and returned the cup to its saucer as the sound of the polished brass door knob was heard turning in the oaken door. Daniel entered meekly as Nathan, having returned to his reading, appeared to take no notice. Standing nervously, he awaited judgement. At length, Nathan lowered his paper and eyed him.

"How are you feeling this morning?"

"Okay, Papa."

"And Washington?"

"Aunt Nettie says he's okay too."

Nathan folded the paper slowly and deliberately, placing it upon the desk. He then leveled his gaze directly at Daniel, studying him closely. Daniel lowered his eyes, unable to endure the scrutiny.

"God and good fortune have placed you in a position of rank, Daniel. But with it comes responsibility. You have failed both yourself, and your family, by treating Washington thusly." Nathan placed his elbows on the desk and leaned forward. "You owe him an apology."

Daniel looked up at his father.

"But Papa... he's..."

"Flesh and blood. With feelings. Just Like you and I," said Nathan firmly.

Daniel's eyes began to well up.

"That was a cruel trick you boys played on him. I might have expected it from the others, but not from you. Tell me... why should he respect you, if you show no respect for him?"

"I'm sorry, Papa."

Nathan studied his son whose head was bowed in shame.

"I will pass on something to you that my father impressed upon me when I was about your age. 'Be firm when it is required, kind when it is not... but above all, be just.'"

Daniel looked up, repentant, tears streaking his face.

"You may go."

Daniel turned to leave.

"But be sure to be back by dinner. They tell me Nettie has a fine rabbit stew planned."

In the horse stable, Wash, plying a long-tanged rake, was busy cleaning out a stall, dumping manure into a wooden wheel barrow. Light showed through the wide vertical pine board slats that comprised the walls of the expansive barn, projecting lines of brightness across the bay, the floor covered with saw dust, illuminating rows of hooks holding tools, headstalls, and lead ropes.

Wash coughed, stopped to wipe his nose on his sleeve, then continued with the rake. Daniel entered the stable at the end of the bay and followed the sound of Wash working, stopping in front of the open stall gate.

"Wash... I'm sorry for what I did to you yesterday. It was a mean thing to do. I come to apologize."

Wash continued to work, as if Daniel wasn't there.

"Wash?"

Wash went on, not looking at him.

"Wash. I'm sorry. Forgive me."

Wash stopped.

"Uncle Gabe tells it's the Lord we got's to go to for forgiveness," he said looking down, the wooden rake handle leaning loosely against his shoulder.

Daniel studied him for a moment, then dropped to his knees, clasping his hands in prayer, a line of sunlight cutting across his closed eyes as he raised his face upward.

"Dear Lord, I humbly ask your forgiveness for the cruel way I treated Wash. It was a mean thing to do leaving him out in that awful storm to maybe catch his death of cold or get forever lost in the wilderness, him being always faithful and never doing anything to deserve being treated such, and I give my solemn promise not to do anything like that to him ever again, so long as I live, so help me God. Amen."

Daniel opened his eyes and looked at Wash.

"Well. If'n the Lord forgives you, I reckon I best too."

Daniel arose and commenced to dig in his pocket for something. Finding it, he held it forward and placed it in Wash's hand. It was the palmetto button. Daniel smiled and turned to head down the bay.

"Marse Dan'l?"

Daniel stopped near the door.

"When we going to the creek again?"

"Today if you want."

Daniel left him holding the brass button in his open palm, shining brilliantly in a striated ray of morning light.

At Robber's hole, Daniel undressed quickly to go for a swim.

"Marse Dan'l!"

Daniel looked up to see Wash standing naked on a rock at the head of the swimming hole, arms outstretched, waving.

"I'm a redcoat. Shoot me!"

Daniel quickly raised his imaginary rifle and took careful aim.

"Pow!"

Wash made a stunned, painful face, grabbed his chest convincingly with one hand, pinched his nose with the other and pitched forward into the water. Popping up laughing, he splashed his way toward Daniel.

CHAPTER NINE
(1860)

Daniel and Wash made their way slowly across a grassy field. It was mid-December and the dry Indian grass crunched beneath their feet as they walked, Daniel with one of the fine English shotguns at the ready, Wash slightly behind and to the right carrying a game bag. Two spaniels, descendants of old Bose, patrolled the field ahead for quail eagerly, tongues out, tails held high. Wash turned his head at the sound of a horse loping toward them from a distance, giving a low whistle to alert Daniel. They both watched as the rider approached at a fast clip, clods of dirt kicking up under the horse's belly, the rider urging his mount on with a swat of his hat to the hindquarters. Coming to a quick stop before them, he dismounted the sweating chestnut mare excitedly, grasping the reins with one hand and raising his hat with the other. It was Joe Fletcher, slight of build, dark haired, sinewy.

"They've done it Daniel! It's final. The legislature voted yesterday to secede. I'm headin' to Columbia to volunteer. They're raising an army as we speak. Bobbie's joining too!"

"Maybe there won't be a fight, Joe."

"Well if there is one, I'm sure not going to miss it."

Joe grinned and swung back up on his lathered mount, whose dancing hooves had continued to lift, eager to continue the run.

"South Carolina needs us Daniel," said Joe as he reined the mare around in a tight choppy spin, then galloped off, leaving Daniel and Wash looking at one another.

Daniel and Wash rode up to the stable and dismounted while the dogs who had been trotting along behind, tongues hanging, made their way to the water trough and, forepaws hooked on the rim, lapped vociferously. Wash took Daniel's reins and led the horses in to be unsaddled and brushed as Daniel, shotgun and game bag in hand made his way around the back of the house toward the kitchen. Inside, Nettie and Julia were busy rolling out dough for a pie crust when Daniel mounted the steps and entered.

"Hey Aunt Nettie. Wash and I got nine this morning," placing the game bag on the side table as he nodded to Julia, who returned a smile.

"Would have done better if we'd stayed out longer. Where is father?"

"In the garden shed honey. Las' I checked."

Nathan, at his workbench was carefully placing wraps on a grafted sapling. The garden shed, one of Nathan's favorite refuges, was lined with pine shelves stocked with glass jars of seeds, cuttings, leaves, nuts, all systematically labeled and numbered, for arboriculture had become one of his chief interests, if not a passion, in the last few years. A growing table ran down the middle upon which laid a myriad of earthen pots containing grafted saplings, all carefully cut, tied, wrapped and planted, while an assortment of tin watering cans filled with mineral enriched waters lined the cinder laden floor beneath. Nathan, putting the final touches on a graft wrap, held it up to the light of one of the open shutters and turned it slowly in his fingers, examining it closely as Daniel entered.

"New variety?"

"A different peach. We'll see. How was the hunting?"

"Fine. Until we were distracted."

"By?"

"News. South Carolina has seceded."

Nathan stopped turning the sapling and, laying it down on the table, removed his spectacles.

"I was afraid of this."

Daniel stepped up to the bench beside Nathan.

"I wish to offer my services Father. I've come to ask your blessing."

Nathan looked out the open shutters.

"You are my only son Daniel. I have grave misgivings about how this will turn out."

"Father, our home is threatened. It's only right that I should help to defend it. Don't you agree?"

Nathan turned to look his son directly in the face, both alarmed and awed by the maturity and earnestness of the boy turned young man before him, his reddish blonde hair in waves, dark eyes flashing.

"Yes. I suppose that is true."

"Besides, I can't imagine this thing going on for very long. It will likely be over before we know it."

Nathan tried to restrain his doubt.

"I would prefer to take Wash with me... if of course it is permissible."

Nathan considered for a moment.

"That would seem prudent. How does he feel about it?"

"Oh, he's adamant."

The evening was cool and pleasant, a light breeze wafting past the drawn brocaded curtains of the parlor windows as Ruth, seated with guitar and Sarah astraddle a cello, embarked upon the opening lines of "The Gentle Maiden". Aunt Nettie and Julia moved through the room serving coffee and cakes to the small group which included Nathan and Sophia, Daniel, Samuel, Sophia's sister Beatrice and her husband George, and Sophia's mother Margaret. Daniel, proud of his sisters' musical accomplishments smiled at Samuel, while George and Beatrice nodded approvingly. Margaret, who had gifted the Ledlows most of the instruments in the parlor to include the harpsichord, placed her hand on Sophia's, lost in the wistful melody. Nathan, clearly moved by the music, placed his cup and saucer on Julia's tray, then rising quietly, left the room, Sophia following his departure with knowing eyes.

Once out on the front porch, Nathan walked to the end and, leaning on the rail, looked off into the night. Though the cool air soothed the heavy feeling in his chest somewhat, the haunting blend of cello and guitar followed him, spurring a host of thoughts, memories, forebodings.

"You okay Marse Nathan?"

Wash, unseen in the shadows, was sitting in a chair against the wall, listening to the music.

"Yes..." said Nathan, startled. "Yes. Of Course."

"Sho' is a nice doin's you all are puttin' on for Marse Dan'l. The Misses... they do play pretty."

Nathan turned to face him.

"Washington. You will take good care of Daniel?"

"Oh, yes suh. Anything he needs. I'll shore do it."

"You know how brash he can be."

Wash smiled, knowingly.

"I understand. He feels it's his duty to do this. I likely would have done the same. But it's also his duty to return home safely."

"I'll do my bes' to see to it, Marse Nathan. You know that."

TRUE GRAY

Nathan turned back to the rail, looking off into the night as the final notes of the duet landed in graceful decrescendo.

"That goes for you too, Washington."

"Yes suh."

CHAPTER TEN

The length of Gervais Street was festooned with ribbons and numerous versions of the blue flag of South Carolina hanging from balconies, posts, from the tops of awnings, on the sticks of the expectant children play marching to-and-fro. A large group of soldiers dressed in newly made gray woolen uniforms milled about in the street, visiting with friends and family, as excited as crusaders about to embark upon a glorious mission. Amid a lengthy line of supply wagons, a negro teamster checked the tightness of a load rope, pulling vigorously with a foot on the side board, then taking the slack with a deftly turned wrap and a knot. Another adjusted the harness of one of the mules. In front of a building with a mansard sign above proclaiming "Quality Grain and Spirits," a number of musicians, black and white, stood in a group bearing cornets, fifes, saxhorns and drums, some tinkering with their instruments, others warming up with random exercises.

Beside the northern boardwalk, Daniel, surrounded by his family to include Uncle Gabe and Aunt Nettie, donned a newly handmade blue gray uniform coat of fine woolen broadcloth, double breasted, with twin rows of bright brass buttons, brocade coursing down the sleeves.

"I do hope you like it dear brother. Sarah and I were up all hours putting on the finishing touches," said Ruth, adjusting his collar.

"They ain't a lying Marse Dan'l. I see'd 'em, busy as bees, sho' 'nough," added Nettie.

Sarah held out her finger to Daniel.

"Poor me. Pricked it near to the bone in the onslaught. First wound in the defense of our noble cause I dare say."

Daniel hugged them both.

"It's first rate. Fits perfectly. How do I look?"

"Like the brave young officer you are," said Sophia, stepping up.

Nathan, reaching inside his breast pocket, pulled out and held forth a small, black, leather bound bible, tied shut with a ribbon.

"From your mother and I. Not so dashing as your new uniform perhaps, but of value nonetheless, especially in trying times."

Daniel took it in his hands, respectfully.

"Carry this with you Daniel... for us."

Daniel nodded and slipped it into the pocket of his vest.

TRUE GRAY

A short distance away Wash was visiting with Julia and Bessie, Julia handing him a cloth wrapped bundle.

"Bacon an' cornbread. Case you two gets hungry."

A dark man in humble clothing with a gray stubble beard stepped up behind Julia.

"Paw-Paw! You made it!"

"Told you he would," said Julia.

"Now don't you go do nothin' crazy boy," said Neptune, giving Wash a hearty embrace. "Them Yankees, they might not be know'd for their good shootin', but their lead stings jus' the same. You make skinny behind a tree when they start that foolishness. You hear?"

Wash grinned.

Daniel was bidding his family farewell when Wash came up with Bessie.

"Marse Dan'l. Bess's got something for us."

Bessie held out two palmetto shaped cockades, made from fine strips of palmetto frond fixed on straight pins.

"Made 'em myself."

"Why Bess, their beautiful," taking one in his hand and admiring it. "We'll wear them with honor, won't we, Wash."

Bessie beamed, then lowered her eyes shyly as she pinned them hastily to their hats.

"Fall in!" called a voice from down the street, as a bugle sounded off.

Townspeople, eagerly awaiting the approach of the Second South Carolina Regiment, lined the length of the street to the east, as the sounds of the band playing "Bonnie Blue Flag" grew in the distance, echoing off the facades of the buildings. As Colonel Kershaw and his adjutant Major Goodwyn appeared at the head of the column astride prancing black horses, the crowd responded with a rippling chatter which grew in intensity with the sounds of approaching heels on cobblestone. Behind them stepped the color guard carrying the South Carolina state flag and the regimental standard followed by "A" Company, led by their Commander and Adjutant, marching eight abreast.

The Ledlows, positioned on the balcony of the Bank building, watched eagerly for Daniel's unit to appear as Uncle Gabe, Aunt Nettie,

TRUE GRAY

Neptune, Julia and Bessie waited on the boardwalk in front of the Cotton Exchange across the street. As the soldiers marched by, spectators waved blue ribbons and handkerchiefs, cheering and calling to their fathers, sons and brothers. With the swell of the music increasing, Sophia and Julia's eyes met as Julia pointed excitedly up the street at the approach of Company "C", the Columbia Grays, at the head of which were riding Captain Wallace, commanding, and his adjutant Lieutenant Daniel Ledlow, astride fine gray horses. The Ledlows let out a cheer as Ruth and Sarah raised handkerchiefs. Nathan took Sophia's hand as they waved support and Godspeed, while the Ledlow servants clapped and shouted encouragement from across the street. From the next balcony, a stunning ivory skinned young woman with black hair blew a kiss of farewell.

As the band came up, they broke into Dixie, ratcheting up the enthusiasm of the crowd while, behind them, marched two ranks of negroes, to include Wash, stepping proudly to the beat of the band.

"Hurrah for our darkey boys!" called someone from the street.

TRUE GRAY

"They can lick the Yanks all by themselves!" yelled another.

At this the crowd erupted in applause, tears running down Sophia's otherwise stoic face, as the sounds of the Second South Carolina Regiment faded off into the distance.

CHAPTER ELEVEN
(July 1861)

A line of confederates quick marched in single file through the tall woods, their feet shuffling in the pulverized dirt turned dust, powdering brogans, pantlegs and bordering foliage alike, the same faded butternut gray. Sinewy broad chested First Sergeant McGee, sporting muttonchops and chevroned sleeves, ran alongside sweating, unbuttoning his jacket as he moved.

"Close it up ... close it up lads!" he shouted as the whistling of an approaching cannonball was heard, followed by the crashing and splintering of the trees overhead.

"Forward. Forward!"

Another cannonball smashed into a large walnut tree trunk sending shards of splintered wood through the file. A soldier clutching his neck, a large splinter of wood having severed his carotid artery, reeled and fell sending spurts of warm salty blood on his friends close by.

At Henry House Hill, Captain Wallace and Daniel, along with Wash mounted on a bay mule, trotted out from the cover of the trees and onto a broad open slope where a panorama of Union soldiers stood five hundred yards away, arrayed for battle, starred and striped banners waving. Captain Wallace wheeled around and, dismounting, motioned with his arm to Daniel.

"Form line of battle!"

"Form line of battle!" shouted Daniel, dismounting likewise and passing the reins of both mounts to Wash. "Quick Wash, take them to the rear."

Wash grabbed the reins and disappeared into the trees at a trot, as Daniel directed the men rushing from the woods, sweating and breathing hard, being urged on by the vocal sergeants. As the men spread out and took position, they adjusted their spacing hastily to extend and join with the companies forming on either side.

Back in the woods, Wash and Corporal Whiting's servant Mabry, struggled to control the panic-stricken mounts of the officers, the lathered horses wild eyed with fear and dancing at the boom and crash of the cannonade having commenced in earnest upon the scene of battle.

On the field, a broad line of Confederates marched down toward the northern line, Captain

Wallace and Daniel at the head of the Columbia Grays.

"Steady Lads. Steady as she goes," yelled First Sergeant McGee following close behind, moving briskly up and down the line.

As cannonballs plowed up the ground around them, the sounds of the Confederate batteries in answer whistled overhead from the hillocks behind. A northern cannon shot cut a soldier completely in two at the waist, the bottom half taking two more steps before tumbling forward in spasms. Another shot took away a soldier's leg as the line continued on, closing in the gaps. Captain Wallace raised his sword for all to see then, wielding it with purpose, sounded the charge. The Columbia Grays broke into a run, raising an unearthly high-pitched yell, surging forward into the widening blue maw that awaited them.

The afternoon sun shone masked and muted by the smoke of the myriad smoldering patches of scorched earth, while dead horses and the bodies of men lay strewn about on the field, some sporadically, some in lines as if systematically formed up and dispatched without ceremony. A broken Union cannon carriage sat askew at an odd angle, a dismembered blue roan still in harness, on its belly, head bowed, muzzle resting in the dust. A Confederate detail combed the field for survivors, loading them on litters and carrying them to high ground to be sorted and taken by ambulance to the rear. Others searched the field for objects of value, flinching uncontrollably at the occasional sound of a gunshot, sign of yet another wounded horse being dispatched.

Evening found the Columbia Grays fussing about their campfires, talking softly and cooking their rations, some writing home, others staring at nothing, trying to shut out the horrors witnessed but a few hours previously. Within the command tent, Captain Wallace and Daniel sat on camp stools at a folding table, going over a hand colored topographic map by the light of a brass patent, kerosene lantern hanging from the center pole. The captain took a draw from his cigar, eyeing the map closely, exuding a narrow stream of smoke, as a medical aid busied himself dressing the captain's bloodied shoulder. The faintest suggestion of a wince on the part of the captain was then followed by the sound of flapping canvas as in entered Wash in the act of removing his hat, smiling, face covered in sweat streaked dust.

"Looks like we got company, suh."

In came Joe Fletcher and Bobbie Hawkins, saluting Captain Wallace.

"Lieutenants Hawkins and Fletcher, sir. Hampton's Artillery, 'A' Battery," said Joe.

Captain Wallace returned the salute awkwardly with his left hand as they gave Daniel a hearty handshake and clap on the back.

"Glad to see you boys made it through okay," said Daniel.

"Looked to us like you all got the worst of it," Joe added, watching as the aid took the final wrap on Wallace's shoulder. "How are you faring sir?"

"Well enough. They just clipped my wing a bit. Burns like holy hell though."

"You will be joining us for mess I trust?" asked Daniel. "Wash has procured two chickens and some turnips."

"Precisely why we're here Lieutenant," replied Bobbie grabbing Wash playfully around the shoulder. "We are sorely in need of a decent cook in 'A' Battery."

Morning found the camp quiet, the men having been allowed to rest in, all but the outlying sentries. Wash, leaning over a smoky fire, removed a blackened tin coffee pot with a rag and set it aside on a rock to cool. From out of the command tent came Daniel, in his shirtsleeves, suspenders loosened, stretching and yawning.

"Mornin', Marse Dan'l. Coffee?"

"Yes please," scratching and making his way to the edge of the woods to urinate.

"How's the Captain?"

"In bad humor. He'll be alright."

Wash lifted the pot lid with the rag and sprinkled in a dash of cool water, regarding it thoughtfully.

"You think the Yankees will try that again?"

"I wouldn't if I were them," said Daniel, returning to the fire, buttoning his pants.

Wash handed him a tin cup of steaming black coffee as Daniel took a seat on a nearby camp stool. Breaking a few sticks over his knee, he added them to the fire.

"They shore made a mess o' things out there."

"Yes. They did indeed," said Daniel, gingerly taking a sip of coffee. "Find anything of value?"

"Yes suh," said Wash, pouring himself a cup and squatting by the fire. "A good pair of wooly socks, a razor, two silk hank-o-chiffs, some ammunition... and a musket."

"Really. What make?"

"Don't know. Has a crown on it. Like a king would wear."

"Well now Wash... that would be an Enfield rifle musket."

"Is that good?"

"Oh yes. What are you going to do with it? Trade it?"

"Jus' a' soon hang on to it if it's okay with you Marse Dan'l. I might want to shoot a Yankee."

Daniel, cradling his tin cup, took another sip of coffee, thinking, as Wash poked at the reviving fire with a stick.

"Well... if you're going to carry it, we had best make sure you know how to use it."

In a grassy clearing well outside of camp, Daniel placed a wild gourd to form the head atop a makeshift man-sized target consisting of a willow pole stuck in the ground, a stick lashed to it crosswise for arms and a burlap grain sack for a body. Satisfied with his efforts, Daniel paced off one hundred yards, counting in his head as Wash followed. Turning back to look at the target, Daniel considered it thoughtfully.

"Now, shooting an infantry rifle musket is considerably different from the shotguns we've hunted with," said Daniel, producing one of the paper cartridges.

Wash took the cartridge in hand and examined it curiously.

"Just bite the end to open it and pour the powder down the barrel."

Wash did so, tipping the paper cylinder into the upright muzzle.

"It will kick quite a bit more than you're used to for one thing, so it's important to just concentrate on the target and not flinch in anticipation."

Wash placed the minie ball over the muzzle as Daniel tore the excess paper away.

"This part just gets thrown aside."

Wash pulled the ram rod out through its ferrules, reversed it, and began pushing the bullet down.

"Make sure it is completely seated, Wash. This can get missed, especially if you're in a hurry, and can result in a blown barrel," said Daniel, handing him a percussion cap. "Now bring it to half cock and cap it."

Wash pulled back the hammer slowly, fitting the copper cap over the nipple, then commenced raising the rifle to his shoulder.

"Just keep the front site in the rear notch and line it up," said Daniel, pointing at the blade and rear site.

Wash pulled to full cock and held down range as Daniel stood intently by.

"Remember. Just hold in the middle. If you hit a man anywhere, he will likely be out of the fight."

Daniel took a step back and watched, arms folded, as Wash held steady and squeezed. The charge touched off with a crack and a recoil, a cloud of acrid white smoke wafting off to the north. A wiggle of the target was noted, but nothing conclusive as Daniel and Wash made their way back down to assess the shot. The gourd was found to be shattered, lying in yellowed bits of shell and foamy pulp on the ground behind. Daniel surveyed the target, taking in the fractured shards of gourd strewn about.

"Were you aiming for the middle of the body?"

"Oh, Marse Dan'l. I thought you meant for the middle of the head."

CHAPTER TWELVE

It had been two months since the northern army was sent reeling back, stung by their encounter with the southerners near the town of Manassas. Amid a thick stand of leafy young willows, two Union soldiers on a probing mission, made their way slowly toward the sound of moving water when the slighter one in the lead stopped short, holding his hand back to halt his companion. Straining to listen, they remained still for several minutes, then crouching low, commenced to move forward, cautiously.

On the opposite bank of the river Wash stood guard as Mabry, wading waist deep, checked a throw line they had set the previous evening.

"Look 'a here Wash," he said, tugging on the linen line. "Another cat. And a good'n too!" Mabry lifted it up, it flipping and fighting in the air, wide headed, whiskery, shiny and brown, shedding water off in sunlit diamonds, looking to spike its captor if at all possible.

The Union soldiers peered through the trees at the gray jacketed enemy who had so foolishly given away their position on the opposite bank.

The leader, kneeling, cocked his Springfield rifle, and took careful aim.

"Be quick to scram Karl, if we stir up a hornet's nest," he said in a whisper.

As Mabry, grinning, made his way toward the bank with his prize, the sharp crack of a rifle sounded, the bullet blowing the catfish to bits before smashing into the muddy bank with a slap.

"Damn," he said, scrambling up the bank.

Wash immediately returned a shot toward the sound of the report.

"Quick Mabe! Make skinny behind a tree."

Another shot thudded into a tree trunk just as Mabry managed to take cover behind it, breathing heavily, still clutching the line and the remains of the catfish head. Wash, jumping behind a boulder, loaded another powder charge and rammed a minie ball home, replacing the rod deftly.

"Soon as I fire, you jump back to another tree," he said lowly, capping the nipple.

Mabry dropped the line and waited stock still, wide eyed, listening for the report. Wash peered through a crevice in the rock and fired, the blue coated leader's hat taken off cleanly by the bullet.

"Whoaa!" he said rolling to the side for cover, feeling of his scalp for traces of blood, while Wash and Mabry darted back to take up new positions ten yards further up from the river.

"Same thing Mabe," whispered Wash as he hastily reloaded. The larger of the two blue coats raised up slightly and blinked.

"Hey. Those boys are colored."

"They're probably just dirty."

"No Wolf. They're colored. I swear it. I saw them." They exchanged looks, pondering this for a moment.

"Hey Johnny!" yelled Wolf across the river. "You boys negroes?"

From the other side, Wash at the ready, peered around his tree looking for a shot.

"What if we are?" he answered back.

"What the hell are you doing fighting for their side? Don't you realize they have you enslaved?"

Wash and Mabry looked at each other from their tenuous defensive positions.

"Well, looks like you're trying to *kill* us!"

Nothing was heard for a few minutes but the gurgling of the moving water.

"Look here," said Wolf. "One of you over there is cutting it a little fine to suit us. How about we just break it off, all gentleman like."

"You first," said Wash.

Wash kept a bead on them as they rose up tentatively and, with heads ducked, disappeared off into the woods.

CHAPTER THIRTEEN
(June 1862)

From a knoll near Savage's Station, east of Richmond, Captain Wallace, mounted, glassed the battlefield with Daniel at his side. In the distance a line of Union artillery could be seen, their mules kicking up dust, maneuvering cannon into place near the crest of a hill a quarter of a mile away, preparing to defend an anticipated Confederate assault. As he continued surveying the scene, the *zing* of a sniper's bullet glanced off of a rock not ten feet away and careened upwards toward the rear, causing both mounts to flinch and toss their heads.

"Damn him," said Captain Wallace, closing the telescope briskly. "Cannot someone silence that man? He is making things considerably more difficult than need be." Irritated, he returned the glass to its leather case. "Who do we have that can deter him?"

"I will dispatch someone immediately sir," said Daniel.

"See to it, then."

A short time later, Wash, well forward of the Confederate line, eyed a tall pine tree and, slinging his Enfield, began climbing quickly, limb by limb. Finding a stable perch and good vantage point thirty feet up, he commenced scanning the enemy position for telltale gunpowder signatures.

Back upon the knoll a courier galloped up to Captain Wallace and Daniel, coming to a quick stop and handing over a message to the Captain with a salute.

"They are covering a retreat sir. Prepare to pursue."

Another sniper bullet slapped the courier's mount in the neck, causing it to crumple forward, the blood-spattered rider deftly jumping clear.

From his position in the pine tree Wash saw a puff of smoke, followed by a lingering report. Bracing against the trunk, he took careful aim at the barely discernable speck that appeared to be the smoke's origin and fired. A wave of Confederates rushed forward then, yelling to beat all hell as an all-out assault commenced. As the gray clad lines pressed on, crowding the enemy, they in turn began their retreat in order, pausing only momentarily to fire random cover shots at their pursuers. Commanding an extraordinary view of the field, Wash watched as the battle unfolded. Cannon shots screamed above while the crack of rifle fire grew in intensity, sending clouds of pungent black powder smoke drifting across the field and up into the tree tops. Dark forms came into view as, through the haze, ran two Yankee soldiers, having been separated from their unit, making haste toward the cover of the woods edge. Reaching the comparative safety of the forest, they stopped momentarily, leaning on a tree to catch their breath, directly below Wash.

In the aftermath of the assault a Confederate, having secured an enemy cannon, checked the carriage for soundness, while another examined the touch hole to see that it hadn't been spiked. Yet another nudged a Yankee artilleryman lying still on his face on a patch of blood-soaked earth, making sure he was dead. With Captain Wallace off to regimental headquarters, Daniel sat at the field table in the company command tent making his battle report, when the sound of footsteps were heard, hesitating at the tent entrance.

"Who's there?" said Daniel placing his pen in the ink stand.

"First Sergeant McGee, Sir."

"Yes, enter please."

Sergeant McGee, ducking to enter, came to attention saluting, then approached withdrawing a gunpowder smudged paper from his coat pocket, unfolding it carefully and holding it forth.

"Sir, eleven dead, sixteen wounded, six unaccounted for."

"I see... and Washington?"

"Among the missing, sir."

Daniel looked down at his report then back up at Mcgee. From without the tent the voice of Corporal Whiting sounded off.

"Prisoners inbound, First Sergeant!"

Outside, soldiers, roused from their rest, stood and gathered to witness the parading through camp of two sullen blue coated prisoners marching unwillingly at the point of Wash's Enfield, their two Spingfields slung across his back.

"Step lively, Billys," he said, nudging the rearmost soldier in the small off his back with the rifle muzzle. "We don't have all day. I'm hungry."

Daniel and Sergeant McGee emerged from the tent in time to see the procession approaching, the amused Columbia Grays hooting and hollering at the plight of the chagrined Yankees. Wash, with an authoritative command, halted them before Daniel.

"Well, what do we have here, Wash?"

"Two less o' them rascals to shoot at us I reckon, Marse Dan'l."

Several shouts of approval were heard amidst the murmur of laughter rippling through the ranks, while Sergeant McGee and Corporal Whiting looked on in amazement.

"Very well then. They shall remain in your charge until such time as we consolidate prisoners."

The blue coats exchanged looks of bewilderment.

"Yes suh!" said Wash, snapping a salute.

Daniel, taken off guard, returned it, surveyed the grinning crowd, then re-entered the tent to complete his report.

Day break two days later found one of the prisoners, a portly sort with a goatee, shirtsleeves rolled up, bent over, cleaning Wash's mule's hooves with a pick. The mule, unaccustomed to the smell of Yankees, brayed and wrenched his rear hoof loose with a snort and a fart.

"Stand still, you ungrateful ass. I'm enjoying this less than you, I can assure you," he said in a low voice, wrestling the hoof back upon his knee, resuming his task. The other prisoner, a lanky blonde Swede, took up his stance alongside a pile of split wood, taking another swing with an axe at an upright junk of elm, balanced on a stump. With a grunt and a thud of the axe, the wood careened off to the side. The Swede, bending to retrieve it, wiped the sweat from his forehead with his sleeve and repositioned the chunk on the block. A second try was more successful as he tossed the split pieces on the pile and rubbed the small of his back. Meanwhile, Wash, sitting on a stool by the fire, smoked his corncob pipe, keeping a watchful eye.

"Now you check them feets close, Billy. We still got some chasin' to do 'fore we're rid of you boys for good," said Wash. Then, turning his commentary on the Swede. "Where'd you learn to use a axe? Don't they chop wood up there in Yankeeville? We're burnin' it faster than you're cuttin' it."

Within the command tent Daniel dipped his pen and wrote a few lines in a letter to home as Captain Wallace snored fitfully in his bunk, seizing a last few precious moments of sleep. First

Sergeant McGee entered quietly, standing and saluting with a wry smile.

"The detail to collect prisoners has arrived sir," he said in a low voice so as not to wake the Captain.

"Very well," said Daniel returning the salute and resuming his letter. Sergeant McGee remained in place.

"Sir... should I inform Washington, or would you prefer to?"

"Ah, yes," said Daniel, rotating the pen in his hand, then placing it down. "I'd best do it."

McGee saluted and exited as Daniel considered his unfinished letter for a moment, glanced toward the sleeping Captain, then rose to leave.

The Swede, using a stick, adjusted the coals of the campfire as the goateed prisoner, breathing heavily, arrived bearing two buckets of water and set them on the ground nearby. Wash, seated on his camp stool, motioned to the stew pot, the Swede dutifully lifting the lid with a hook and stirring the simmering contents with a wooden spoon. Satisfied with the stew's progress, he replaced the lid and rehung the spoon on the blackened iron spit as Daniel approached.

"Mornin' Marse Dan'l," said Wash jumping up to offer his seat, while motioning to the goateed one who promptly fetched another stool and placed it for Wash.

"I'm finishing a letter to home. Any words you would like included?" asked Daniel, stretching his boots toward the fire. Wash thought as he knocked out his pipe and began refilling it from a cloth sack taken from his britches pocket.

"Yessuh. Give my best to everybody," pressing the tobacco down gently with his thumb, "and thank Aunt Nettie, Mama and Bess for the molasses candy. Sho' was good... while it lasted."

"Okay."

Wash snapped his finger toward the Swede who brought a burning stick from the fire, holding it carefully for Wash to relight his corncob.

"Did you tell 'em 'bout my Yankee prisoners?" Wash asked, puffing his pipe to life, then waving the Swede away.

"Yes, as a matter of fact."

"Sho'ly would love to see Paw-Paw's face when he hears 'bout that."

Daniel looked at the two prisoners who stood by, uncomfortably awaiting orders.

"Wash, I'm afraid they will be gathering them up for transport to the rear this morning."

"But Marse Dan'l. I was just now gettin' 'em trained right."

Daniel shrugged with a sympathetic smile, as Wash puffed on his pipe in reflection.

"Well now...that is a shame," he said looking at his prisoners. "I sho' do see how a fellow could get used to this alright."

Six weeks after the successful route of the Yankees at Savage's Station, the Columbia Grays found themselves encamped toward evening, within hearing of the rippling Rappahannock. A group of ten or so soldiers relaxed around a campfire listening to Corporal Whiting clawhammer lightly on fretless banjo, he having just finished tacking on a new head repurposed from a field drum, the unwilling gift of a nearby regimental band. Beneath the spreading canvas fly of the command tent, Daniel and Captain Wallace relaxed in folding camp chairs, smoking pipes and listening on.

"How much longer do you think they will continue this fight, Sir?" said Daniel knocking out his pipe and refilling it from a cannister on the ground between them.

"Not much longer I should think, given their success rate thus far. Why? Are you tiring of the show?"

"No sir. Not at all. But I would be guilty of an untruth were I to say there were perhaps not other pursuits I might prefer."

"Such as?"

"Well, the home plantation for one. I am the only son. I worry about Father trying to keep everything running by himself."

Captain Wallace took a long puff on his cherry wood pipe, the bowl glowing in the twilight, slowly exuding an aromatic plume of Virginia tobacco which rose gently, bunching up against the top of the tent fly before spilling off into the evening.

"I dare say Lieutenant... it would seem that there might perhaps be the influence of a member of the fairer sex in play here."

"Perhaps sir," said Daniel, glad the light was failing.

"Perhaps? No most certainly so," said the Captain, as if successfully turning an adversary's flank. "Pretty I should think?"

"Prettiest in Columbia, sir."

Captain Wallace smiled, recalling for a moment a lost image from his youth.

"Yes. Yes, of course. A young woman befitting of the Adjutant of the Columbia Grays."

Breaking the silence, came Wash's rich deep voice from the direction of the campfire, singing a familiar song.

> As time draws near my dearest dear,
> when you and I must part.
> How little you know of the grief and woe,
> in my poor aching heart.
>
> 'tis but I suffer for your sake,
> believe me girl it's true.
> I wish that you could go with me,
> or I was staying with you.
>
> I wish my breast were made of glass,
> wherein you might behold.
> Upon my heart your name lies wrote,
> in letters made of gold.

TRUE GRAY

In letters made of gold my love,
believe me when I say,
you are the one I will adore,
until my dying day.

Captain Wallace unstopped a silver flask pulled from his vest pocket, took a swig, and offered it to Daniel. Daniel in turn took a drink, the smoky amber whiskey, a southern sacrament to the past, present, and future, and handed it back as Wash's voice continued on.

The blackest crow that ever flew,
would surely turn to white,
If ever I proved false to you,
bright day would turn to night.

Bright day would turn to night my love,
the elements would mourn,
If ever I proved false to you,
the seas would rage and burn.

The song ended giving way to silence, save the crackling of dry sticks on the campfire, followed by the wistful applause of Wash's soldier audience.

"Hey Johnny!" sounded a voice from far off in the night. "Send out your baritone!"

In moments a number of Confederates including Daniel and Wash, under cover of the trees near the river bank, peered across the waters into the darkness, searching for the source of the request.

"Send out your baritone, Johnny! We want to hear him," exclaimed the hidden voice once more. Daniel looked to Wash in the low light of the rising moon.

"We would, but we are afraid you might ruin his jacket."

The low murmur of voices was heard, barely audible from across the water, followed by the sounds of bending branches as several forms emerged from the trees, showing themselves in the moonlight upon the far bank, a trio of Union soldiers. As the group of Grays watched guardedly, the Yankees commenced to sing in tight three-part harmony.

Way down upon the Suwanee River,
far, far away.
There's where my heart is turnin' ever,
there's where the old folks stay.

All up and down the whole creation,
sadly I roam.
Still longing for the old plantation,
and for the old folks at home.

The Confederates exchanged looks of surprise as the blue coated singers doubled down on the chorus.

All the world is sad and dreary,
everywhere I roam.
Oh, darkeys how my heart grows weary...

The trio held a coda, then landed their performance dramatically with a flourish.

... far from the old folks at home.

The Grays, having gained in strength along the edge of the tree line, erupted with claps and Rebel yells, as the Yankees took a gentlemanly bow. As the commotion began to die down, the trio remained, waiting expectantly. Wash looked questioningly to Daniel, who nodded his approval. With nothing to break the quiet then but the sporadic chirping of crickets, the northerners watched as a lone Rebel stepped out from the trees and made his way down to the water. Taking up his place on a gravel bank, he removed his straw hat in the pale moonlight, revealing his color, and commenced to sing.

> *John Brown's body lies a moulderin'*
> *in the grave,*
> *John Brown's body lies a moulderin'*
> *in the grave,*
> *John Brown's body lies a moulderin'*
> *in the grave,*
> *But his soul is marching on.*

> *He's gone to be a soldier in the army*
> *of the Lord,*
> *He's gone to be a soldier in the army*
> *of the Lord,*
> *He's gone to be a soldier in the army*
> *of the Lord,*
> *His soul is marching on.*

The Union trio witnessed the scene in wonder, as Wash reached powerfully from down deep.

> *Glory, glory hallelujah,*
> *Glory, glory hallelujah,*
> *Glory, glory hallelujah,*
> *His soul is marching on.*

As the last note ended in a lingering fade, wafting off into the trees, settling down atop the drifting waters, melting away into the night, Wash waited, stock still beneath the moon, hat in hand, unsure of what to expect. For what seemed an eternity, the Union soldiers stood in silence, transfixed. At last the leader stepped forward and doffed his hat, the others following suit, as they turned quietly and disappeared into the woods from whence they had come.

CHAPTER FOURTEEN
(September 1862)

The sky was dark as if in eclipse, the air thick with gun smoke, as the Columbia Grays slammed headlong into an advancing line of Yankees near Dunker Church. As the enemy fired a volley and rushed to meet the charge, thirteen Confederates fell, crumpling forward. A northern cannonball bounced its way through the ranks, grazing Captain Wallace, who twisted and dropped, clutching at his shattered ribs. Daniel, close by, rushed to his side, assessed the situation in seconds, and assumed command in a desperate attempt to prevent a rout.

A quarter mile back in the woods Wash and Mabry tended the officer's mounts, listening intently to the sounds of the raging battle. Through the trees came a wounded bay horse, wide eyed, hobbling awkwardly, trailing a foreleg by a tendon. Wounded men then approached, making their way through the trees, bleeding, limping, one holding his arm tightly against his chest, having lost a hand. Another held a wad of torn, blood-soaked shirt against the side of his head where his ear had been.

"They're whippin' us boys! Where's our reinforcements? We gotta stop 'em!"

Wash, gazing upon the soldier's bloodied gray jacket, handed his reins off to Mabry, shouldered his Enfield, and struck a trot.

Near the edge of the woods Daniel addressed the remainder of the Gray's, sweating and heaving, some kneeling, others leaning back against the pine trunks, winded from the hard, running fight to the trees.

"They're over extended men. We've got them in a trap. I need every last one of you with me now. When I give the charge, we'll show them what the sharp end of a palmetto stake looks like! Are you with me?"

Daniel surveyed the grim eyed, powder blackened visages of his company's survivors, assessing their resolve. Standing among the ranks was Wash, his rifle at the ready. Daniel drew his sword.

"Forward!" he yelled motioning back toward the horrible din of battle.

The Grays followed in order through the woods, the shrieking sounds of rifle and cannon fire deafening, as they approached the edge of the tree line. Two hundred yards away, across the littered field, the Union ranks advanced obliquely in force, tattered flags flying. Daniel at the head of the Grays, brandished his sword.

"Give it to 'em boys!" he shouted, as a piercing Rebel yell erupted, the Columbia Grays bolting from the woods, pitching into the flank of the Union ranks with a vengeance.

Two days later Daniel, leaning over the field table, penned the finishing lines of the battle report, then standing, cast his eyes toward the empty end of the command tent and ducked out for the night air. By the light of the campfire, Wash busied himself sewing a patch of jean cloth over a hole in his straw hat, as Daniel approached and pulled up a stool.

"What's that?"

"Yanks tried to put a vent in my skull, Marse Dan'l," said Wash, pulled from his thoughts, holding his bullet pierced hat out for Daniel's inspection. He took another stitch with the bone needle, pulling a length of salvaged woolen yarn through to the inside of the sweat stained crown. "Shame 'bout the Cap'n. He might 'o been cantankerous, but he was good... and brave." Wash angled his hat to capture the fire light as he poked the needled back through. "They goin' to promote you?"

"It would appear so."

"Well now. That's fine," said Wash, exhibiting pride. "Cap'n Marse Dan'l!"

Daniel smiled faintly, turning his gaze toward the fire.

"You did good the other day."

"They jus' keep comin'," Wash said, shrugging and continuing his mending. "How many do you reckon there are?"

Daniel pondered, then discarded, the perplexing question as the hoofbeats of a courier were heard, trotting by in the night. Wash, pulling the last stitch through, made a knot, storing the needle in his frayed coat lapel, and rotated the hat in his hands, assessing his work.

"Wash?"

Wash looked at Daniel, questioningly.

"I realize, with all this commotion going on, you could leave and head north at any time."

"Why would I do that?"

"Others have. I wouldn't blame you if you did."

Wash looked into the fire, then back at Daniel.

TRUE GRAY

"I couldn't do that, Marse Dan'l. The South is my home, same as you. All my family and friends. The North is no place for me." He placed his hat on his head. "Besides, it's too damn cold up there... and I hear tell the food tastes funny."

Daniel studied Wash for a moment, then conceded with a smile.

A two weeks march had brought the Grays to a new camp, hilly and thick with poplars, an abundance of fire wood and a reasonably close source of water. Wash, the sleeves of his coarsely woven indigo shirt rolled up, worked at a tub of hot water with a wad of burlap, scrubbing the months-worth of soot and blackened matter that had accumulated on the assortment of pots and skillets lying about on the ground nearby. Giving the stew pot a last dunk and swirl in the hot water, Wash laid it aside and reached for a tin pan as Mabry trotted up excitedly.

"Blackberries Wash! Bunches. I done run into a whole big patch of 'em."

With Mabry's help the pots were put in order and set out to dry in the sun, as Wash, shouldering his Enfield, followed Mabry off through the woods northward toward the blackberry motherlode. Just as Mabry had reported, the thorny bushes were loaded with berries, dark and plump, practically untouched as of yet by the wild birds, badgers and foxes that inhabited the forest. Leaning his rifle on a tree, Wash and Mabry fell to picking, filling their haversacks in short order, barely making a dent in the bountiful harvest.

"I wasn't a lying now was I Wash," said Mabry hefting his bag, blue black stains beginning to show through the dirty, cream-colored canvas from the press of fruit. "We ain't even close to bringing the crop in, is we?"

"You haul 'em back Mabe," said Wash, handing him his haversack, "and bring back whatever you can find... buckets, blankets, anything. We'll fix blackberry cobbler 'nough for the whole company."

Mabry shouldered the sacks of fruit and headed back to camp at a trot as Wash continued to pick enthusiastically, tossing berries into his upturned hat crown. Following a thicket of brambles up a rise, picking happily, he suddenly heard something akin to the snapping of a twig, though not quite the same. Raising and turning to look, he found himself at once face to face with three Union soldiers, rifles pointed and cocked.

Daniel and Joe Fletcher sat beneath the command tent fly at mid-day, smoking pipes and conversing.

"Poor Bobbie," said Daniel, shaking his head. "Did he suffer much?"

"We can only pray not. It was a horrible wound. Canister. By the time I reached him, he was gone. A detail was dispatched to take him home."

Daniel, taking a draw from his pipe, let his mind drift for a spell, seeing Bobbie as when they had first met as boys, the three of them running the woods near Peach Creek.

"So, what now?"

Joe looked at him through the pipe smoke.

"Our battery was decimated. Scarcely a third of us left. There is talk of either reforming or attaching us to other units."

Daniel nodded, reflecting upon the gravity of Joe's situation.

"I don't suppose you could use an adjutant?" asked Joe.

The gruff clearing of a voice was heard from a distance as First Sergeant McGee approached at a quick step with Mabry in tow. Arriving before them he stopped short and delivered a quick salute, Mabry doing likewise.

"Sir, Captain Ledlow sir, it would appear Washington has gone missing, sir."

"Missing?"

"We was pickin' berries, suh," added Mabry. "When I went back for him he was gone. All but his rifle."

Daniel, taking a moment to digest the news, tapped his pipe out on his heel and rose to his feet.

"Form a detail. We will conduct a search immediately. Something has befallen him."

"Yes sir. Straight away," said McGee, saluting and turning on his heels, Mabry following.

In the woods amidst the thorny patch, four soldiers stood guard as Daniel, Joe, Sergeant McGee and Mabry examined the ground where Wash had last been seen. Footprints could be discerned approaching from the northeast, along with those of Wash and Mabry in their wanderings through the brambles. Wash's berry stained hat lay askew in the brush, some of the fruit still inside.

"This over here," said Mabry, pointing to the base of a gnarled oak tree, "is where I picked up his rifle an' brought it back 'fore no Yank could get it."

Sergeant McGee, having taken one last turn through the area, returned to the group.

"I don't see signs of a scuffle, sir."

"That's not like him. He would have fought to get away, given a chance."

First Sergeant McGee and Joe exchanged a painful look.

Daniel, studying a map closely by lantern light, stopped, rubbed his brow, and sat back momentarily, thinking. As he reflected upon Wash's Enfield hanging by its sling from a tent pole in the corner, footsteps approached, those of Lieutenant Joe Fletcher, having been made Adjutant of the Gray's three days prior. Entering, he stood quietly beside Daniel and gazed upon the topographical map, worn, having endured repeated rains and folds, marked with pencil, powder, blood and dirt.

"It is rumored we will be pulling back toward Richmond soon."

"Yes," replied Daniel, roused from his thoughts. "That would be my guess."

Joe brought up a field chair and sat down.

"He is gone, Daniel."

Daniel ran his fingers along the frayed edge of the map, as if to heal the splits and torn places.

"Either he turned or was captured. If he in fact turned, things will go easier for him up there. You want what's best for him, don't you?"

"Yes. Yes, of course. I'm... I'm just not ready to accept that he..."

"My friend," said Joe, holding his shoulder. "Wash did more, way more, than any one of us could have expected. He is only human."

Daniel looked Joe in the eye.

"You think he defected?"

Joe gazed upon the Enfield for a moment, then returned a look of sad resignation.

CHAPTER FIFTEEN

Inside a two-acre palisade enclosure near Warrenton, Maryland, Confederate prisoners milled about under guard, while others lay in the shade of the twelve-foot-high log wall on the southern end, trying to nap. Two Union guards posted at the gate smoked and conversed. Just outside of the stockade sat a thickly bearded sergeant and his bespectacled clerk at a rough sawn, pine plank table, the clerk busily making entries in a black, cloth bound ledger, while a guarded group of twenty or so southern prisoners stood in a line, tired, sullen, apprehensive, waiting to be logged in. Having finished with the first, the guards directed him unceremoniously inside the walls.

"Next," growled the bearded sergeant impatiently as up stepped Wash, hatless, the worn cuffs of his gray jacket stained with blackberry juice, the sergeant eyeing him with curiosity.

"Name?"

"Washington."

"First?" asked the sergeant.

"Tha's it. Washington."

The near-sighted clerk glanced at the sergeant, quizzically.

"Last then."

"Ledlow."

"Spell it."

"L... e... d... l... o... w," said Wash, the clerk penning the entry.

"Unit?" asked the sergeant.

"Company "C", Columbia Grays, Second Palmetto Regiment, Army of Northern Virginia."

"Rank?"

"None."

"Yes. Of course," said the sergeant with a sidewise smile at the clerk, stroking his beard, then returning his gaze up at Wash. "Look here Johnny. We have orders to allow you colored boys the opportunity to cross over. We'll get you up in a new blue uniform, with provisions and pay almost as much as the rest. All that is required is for you to take a solemn oath of allegiance to the Union, and of course to disavow the Confederacy."

"No suh, don't believe I'll be doin' that."

"What? Are you mad?" said the sergeant, taken aback. "You look like you haven't had a decent meal in months."

"If you're tryin' to get me to go back on my folks, the answer is no. I won't do it."

The clerk fiddled with his pen awkwardly, aware of the irritation welling up within the sergeant.

"Well," said the sergeant pushing back from the table abruptly and folding his arms, "looks to me like you're just too God damned ignorant to be free. Throw him in with the rest!" he growled to the guards.

Mabry sat on the ground beneath a tree working with needle and thread on the collar of a uniform coat. It had been three days since Wash's disappearance and things were abuzz in camp, the hitching of wagons, the loading of boxes, bundles of canvas, barrels of water, the occasional stamp of a hoof. A bugle sounded off nearby as Mabry broke off the thread and checked his work. The seventy or so soldiers of Company "C", many shoeless, began hurriedly assembling into ranks under the stern direction of First Sergeant McGee and his three staff sergeants. Several mules stood near the wagons, snorting as their packs were tightened. Nearby stood Daniel and Joe talking as their mounts, brushed and saddled, were led up by two orderlies. Mabry came trotting up with the coat then, smiling.

"Here you is, suh," he said, holding it out for Daniel to slip into. "All official and everythin'."

"Thank you Mabe," said Daniel, donning the coat. "Looks mighty fine."

With Mabry's assistance, he fastened the long rows of buttons, finishing near the top where the newly sewn gold, embroidered, triple bars showed to good effect on the collar. Mabry stood back smiling with pride as the orderlies held the bridles for Daniel and Joe to mount. Securing his boots in the stirrups, Daniel turned to Joe.

"Forward Lieutenant."

"Yes Captain," said Joe snapping a salute. "Sergeant McGee... forward!"

The Columbia Grays, set into motion, started out on the march, Daniel and Joe at the head.

A line of weary, ragged Confederate prisoners filed past a steaming black iron pot, suspended from a tripod, as a Union cook in a dirty canvas apron ladled watery gruel into their awaiting tin cups. A second soldier stood by, tearing small chunks of stale bread with his hands and either handing them or dropping them into the extended cups of the inmates as they passed. Wash, receiving his, wandered off to search for a spot in the dry dusty yard on which to sit and eat. After a few moments, a smallish red-haired prisoner with freckles and a slight limp, arose from his place near a comrade who had begun a coughing fit and made his way over near Wash, sitting down cross legged. As they continued to down the tasteless mush, half drinking, half sopping it up with the dry, stale bread, the coughing of the prisoner's comrade gradually subsided, the sufferer laying back on the ground, sweating, exhausted.

"I was right behind you when they herded us in," said the red head, not making eye contact. Wash, guarded, continued to eat.

"Admired the way you set that blue belly back on his heels."

Wash gnawed off a bite of bread and chewed, giving the speaker a quick glance.

"Name's Hubbard. Jim Hubbard, Georgia Rifles. That one over there," motioning carefully with a nod toward the one laying on his back, "is my partner Will Stockett. We was captured at the bridge."

"Wash. Columbia Grays."

Jim exchanged a look with Will who had turned his head slightly in their direction.

"This place'll be the death of him lest I get him out. We plan to make a try of it soon as possible." Jim wiped the last of the gruel out of his cup with his bread. "You in?"

Wash glanced toward Will who was back to looking at the sky, pale, sweating, breathing heavily.

"Yeh. I'm in."

Several prisoners sat on the ground a week later, playing a made up game with buckeyes for pieces, while a Union soldier, leaning with a rifle near the enclosure gate, watched disinterestedly between yawns. About fifty feet away sat Wash against a tree stump, thinking, when Jim and Will walked up lazily in his direction and sat down a short distance away.

"Will and me been studyin' the guards," Jim said in a low voice. "That one that's on duty now is the laziest of the bunch. They rotate shifts and we think we got the schedule figured. He'll never make it through a night post without dozin'."

Wash glanced at the guard discretely.

"How we getting' out?"

"Think you're strong enough to climb over?"

"Probably."

"Well, I'm pretty sure I can too, but my partner here is weakenin' by the day. We'll need to get him over first."

"When?"

"Tomorrow night."

Wash looked at the sky momentarily, then over toward the two, Will smiling sadly, arms folded with palms flat against his sides as if supporting his lungs. Returning his gaze then back to the ground before him, Wash nodded assent.

"Bless you my friend," said Jim.

In the guard house the following night Captain Lawrence, pacing back and forth, stopped at the table and, picking up a small tin cup, drank the contents, then refilled it from a brandy bottle pulled from the drawer. Agitated, he sat down rubbing his brow, when a knock was heard on the door.

"You may enter."

Tall, amber whiskered, Staff Sergeant Elliot entered and coming to attention, saluted. "We've got them in hand sir."

"Good. Where were they apprehended?"

"Not five hundred yards from the wall, Sir. The fools were trying to carry a friend."

"Teach them a lesson Sergeant, then chain them. We must make an example. I will not have this. Do you understand me?"

"Yes sir."

"And place whoever was on guard duty in confinement."

"Already done sir," said Sergeant Elliot.

Wash, Jim and Will were herded by three soldiers into a filthy, ten by ten-foot spiked log jail at the point of a rifle. Weak from the exertion and the beatings, Will stalled at the entrance trying to negotiate the threshold in the dim light of a lantern held by Sergeant Elliot, when he was shoved headlong, sprawling onto the urine and feces saturated earthen floor with a groan.

"Get in you bloody rebel," said one of the guards, kicking him in the sides, rolling him toward the far wall. While two soldiers held rifles on them, the third secured them to the wall by heavy iron clevises hammered into the logs at head level. The prisoners sufficiently shackled, Sergeant Elliott held the lantern up to survey the would-be escapees, their faces swollen and bloody. Will, his hair a reddish clotted matt, slumped in the chains, struggling to breath while Jim, with broken teeth, gazed back, dazed but defiant. In the middle was Wash, one eye swollen shut, blood flowing freely from his nose.

"What's this?" said Sergeant Elliott, holding the lantern closer. "A colored?"

Wash blinked into the lamplight through his good eye.

"Guess this is nothing new for you heh? Being chained and beaten."

The soldiers chuckled at the thought, as Elliott continued to study him.

"To tell the truth suh, it's my first time."

Morning broke cold and cloudy at the prison camp as thinning Confederates wandered piecemeal, stretching and rubbing sore joints, awaiting the feeble breakfast of black coffee and toast being made ready at the north end of the yard. It had been two weeks since any of the inmates had seen the three who had made an attempt at the wall, and rumors and speculations abounded as to their condition or if in fact they were even still in the log jail, or perhaps had been secreted off in the night to be dispatched. As the prisoners began to line up at the kettle, a soldier made his way toward the jail carrying a wooden bucket of water with a dipper and a small cloth bundle of hard tack. Setting the bucket down by the door, he fumbled with a large key, turning it in the iron lock, then lifting the bucket once more, pushed the door open with his brogan. Inside, Wash and Jim squinted, hollow eyed in the morning light which hit them full faced through the open doorway. Will remained slumped in his shackles, unmoving. The soldier, setting the bucket on the floor reached forward tentatively and touched him. Dropping the bundle, he exited nervously and made his way toward the guard house.

As a detail of two soldiers unchained Will Stockett's lifeless body and carried him out by his hands and feet, Sergeant Elliott, along with a guard, entered. Jim's head was down, weak, exhausted, seemingly beaten, While Wash watched, guarded.

"So," said Elliott, "have you two enemies of the state learned anything at all from your little stint here?"

Wash remained silent, returning a gaunt stare.

"No? Perhaps you would prefer to die here in this filth like your mongrel friend," he said, stepping closer to Jim. "What about you, Johnny?"

Jim raised his head slowly and tried in vain to spit, but was too dehydrated to make any.

"Animals!" said Sergeant Elliott, backhanding him. "We are dealing with animals here. Well you can both rot in this place for all I care."

The guard held the door as Sergeant Elliott turned to leave.

"I have suh."

"Pardon me?" said Elliott, stopping short.

"I have," Wash said, looking at him sadly. "I've learned somethin'. I'll take your oath."

Jim turned his head toward him in despair, deserted, defeated.

In the chill of a winter morning, a line of five soldiers in blue wool tunics stood at attention with axes and shovels in front of the guard house, awaiting their orders from Corporal Schmidt. Among them stood Wash.

"Palisade detail boys. We've got nearly three hundred yards of wall to check before sundown. Any tree branches close are to be cut down and dragged away to be burned. Any eroded places will be filled in with rocks hauled up from the pit," said the Corporal walking to and fro as if commanding a line of battle. "Right... face! Forward... march!"

The detail filed out in route step, shovels and axes on their shoulders, past the guard who shut the large hinged double gate behind them. Once outside the men fanned out, working their way along the vertically laid log wall of the perimeter. At a low area, two soldiers busied themselves stacking rocks, tamping them firmly against the base of the wall. A few paces farther down, a soldier tugged at a drooping branch, while another hacked away at it with an axe. Wash, out ahead, shovel in hand, worked his way along the perimeter, looking for branches, compromised earth, tapping logs randomly. At one slightly off colored log, his shovel rebounded with a soft thud. Tapping it again it broke loose slightly from its base, apparently rotted hollow up to about eighteen inches or so. Glancing quickly down the line, he could see Corporal Schmidt chiding two of the soldiers for their ham-fisted handling of a limb. Quickly snapping a stick of dead wood, he wedged the weak log back in place, then grabbing a handful of dirt and spitting into it to make it moist, daubed it carefully over the break line.

"Hey there! You! Get back here and help these dummkopfs!" yelled Schmidt.

"Yes suh, Corporal! Right away!"

Wash grabbed a sprig of laurel and poked it through the logs alongside his repair, then trotted back toward the detail, shovel in hand.

Night time found Sergeant Elliott seated just inside the door of the guard house by the patent iron stove, fighting off a bout of drowsiness, perusing a well-worn copy of *Harper's Weekly* by the dim light of a kerosene lantern hung from a hook in the wall. A north wind gusting in spurts, changed the sound of the stove from a smoky silence to a roar, the base of the blackened stove pipe showing a dull red in the low light. A rap on the door roused him as he cracked it open, the light from within illuminating Private Hendrix's youthful face.

"Here to relieve the guard, Sergeant."

"Very well. About your duty," said Elliott, bringing the door to with a shiver. Rising to retrieve another split chunk of firewood from the box, he opened the stove with a lid hook, poked the wood in and shut it. Hanging the hook on the wood box, he returned to his reading.

A half hour later, Sergeant Elliott was dozing, head down on his chest, the *Harper's* laying limply across his lap, the fire in the stove continuing its slow undulating metre. Barely perceivable, the iron latch began to slide, the door drifting slowly open as a dark figure leaned forward in the dim light of the almost exhausted lantern and lifted the ring of keys from Sergeant Elliott's belt. With no more substance than a puff of smoke from the stove, the figure was gone, the door having been eased soundlessly shut.

In the rank darkness of the log jail, Jim Hubbard was suddenly awakened by a hand clamped firmly over his mouth.

"Shhhh... it's me... Wash."

Jim's heartbeat raced as Wash, trying several keys in the dark, finally succeeded in unlocking him.

"Can you walk?" he asked in a whisper.

"Yeh. Think so."

Once outside, Wash led him as quickly as his stiff legs could manage, across the prison yard in the chilled darkness. Midway across Jim stumbled to his knees, Wash lifting him back to his feet as they continued on. Private Hendrix at his post by the gate, shaken momentarily from his boredom by a strange sound, perked his ears, listening intently. The sound, whatever it might have been, did not repeat however, though it served to put him on edge. Once at the opposite wall, Wash felt feverishly for the laurel sprig he had used to mark the escape opening. Finding it, he waited for a gust of wind, then heaved at the base of the log, it giving way with a muffled thud.

"Halt! Who goes there?" shouted Private Hendrix, running toward the sound. Sergeant Elliott, awakened with a start, jumped to his feet reaching in vain for his keys. Wash, having scrambled through the opening, pulled Jim through by his hands and got him to his feet as they struck for the river. In moments the gate burst open as Hendrix and three other Union soldiers poured out in pursuit. Once at the river bank Jim dropped to his knees to catch his breath, the ominous ripple of the icy waters clipping by before them in the darkness. Their pursuers could be heard yelling and crashing through the woods not a hundred yards behind them.

"Go on Wash! I'm too weak to swim," said Jim, his chest heaving with the exertion.

"Jus' hold on to me. I'll pull you across. C'mon!"

As Jim struggled to his feet, two soldiers suddenly broke out onto the bank thirty yards up stream, took aim and fired, dropping him to the ground with a shot in the back. Instantly Wash dove into the icy cold river and pulled down stream underwater, making the most of his powerful strokes, holding his breath till he felt his lungs would burst. Reloading as they ran down along the bank, the soldiers looked for splashes to shoot at. Fifty feet down stream they got what they hoped for, Wash popping up for a quick breath, then plunging back below, just as shots rang out, coursing through the water.

"We get him?" yelled one, as they made haste to the spot upon which they had fired, straining their eyesight in vain for evidence of the wounded traitor.

"Come on," yelled the other, taking off at a run-down river as the first followed. "He's got to come up sometime!"

The sounds of the soldiers crashing through the shrubs and canes along the bank receded into the distance as Wash having doubled back emerged under some overhanging branches on the opposite shore, gasping for breath. Moments later he sprang from the water and struck a trot southward through the woods, the song "Run Mourner Run" seeming to enter his soul, filling his mind, setting his feet apace, as wet and chilled to the bone, he ran for his life. A Union picket on the far side of the river, having heard the alarm, ran toward the scene. Wash darted past him in the darkness, cutting zig zags as the sentry turned and fired a shot. Unharmed, he picked up the pace. Reaching a stacked rock wall, he vaulted over and hit the ground running across a rutted road and then back into thick woods, the sound of the sentry pursuing in the distance. Minutes later he tumbled headlong into an unseen ravine. Recovering his wits, he gained his feet and scaled a steep bank, covered in thorny brambles, tearing his clothes and flesh.

Once at the top, Wash took flight again across an open field, the sky cloudy and ominous, but the shadow of a moon beginning to show. A covey of roosting guinea hens scattered as he approached, scurrying and flapping in the night. Having reached the far side of the field, he encountered an old split rail fence, slid through and continued into a thick stand of tall trees, forging ahead, hands outstretched before him to fend off trunks as he trotted in the darkness. Out of nowhere a farmer's corn crib appeared, Wash coming up against it with a thud. A dog set to barking as he swung wide of the crib and struck off across a fallow field, stumbling across the plowed furrows. Reaching the extent of the field and pushing though a hedgerow, he found himself in a rutted road. Glancing upward through the trees at the pale moon, Wash chose his direction and trotted on.

The first light of predawn began to illuminate the woods bordering the road as Wash slowed from a trot to a walk, eyeing a gray, slab boarded barn off in the woods to the west. Stopping momentarily to catch his breath, he weighed his options as icy fog lingered about his nose and mouth, rising gently in the still air. With an eye to the impending sunrise, he estimated he had been on the run for nearly seven hours. Tired to the extreme, he made for the barn. Once inside, several hens adjusted themselves, clucking softly, unsure of the intrusion. Pulling the door to, he gently lifted several eggs from their boxes, cracked them, and sucked them down, as he took in the surroundings, rakes and hoes, shovels and scythes. A mule drawn plow rested against the far wall next to a corn crib full of dried ears. He grabbed several ears, stuffing them in his coat pocket, then eyeing a haystack, wriggled his way inside, shivering, exhausted.

The barn door swung open an hour later as the full rays of the morning sun burst forth within, followed by the silhouetted form of a farmer wheeling his cart. Grabbing a pitchfork from the wall, he went about his morning chores which began by loading hay into the cart to be taken to the milk cows in a nearby shed. Quick on his heels rushed his mongrel dog, sniffing about on his normal rounds as the farmer applied the fork aggressively, eager to get the feeding done in the frosty morning air. The dog, suddenly picking up a scent, alerted on the haystack.

"What is it Boozer? Go on. Get it and get gone. We've got work to do," he said, pausing to lean on his pitchfork.

Boozer continued to bark and paw at the haystack, frothing, moving back and forth, his tail at the alert. Suddenly a large black rat scampered out along the wall, Boozer pouncing and seizing its writhing body instantaneously in his jaws. Giving it a quick shake, he bolted out the door with his prize. At this the farmer chuckled and resumed his task, pitching hay into his cart. Finished at length, he hung the pitch fork back in its place and, seizing the ash handles of the cart, wheeled it out, shutting the barn door behind him. In the splintered light of the barn, a bright red rivulet of blood wound its way from beneath the haystack, pooling upon the cold, rough-hewn planks of the barn floor.

CHAPTER SIXTEEN
(December 1862)

A dense morning fog lay thick in a stand of woods west of the town of Fredericksburg, masking the forms of the tree trunks which seemed to loom in staggered ghostly ranks, fading to nothing in the distance. As roosting sparrows commenced to roust and flit about, the cadenced sound of shuffling feet began to be heard, amplifying gradually as if the ghost trunks themselves had taken the notion to move in concert. Through the fog appeared the Columbia Grays, voiceless, quick timing, silent but for the ceaseless shuffle and the breathing. A young soldier stopped momentarily to vomit.

"That's it laddie," said First Sergeant McGee in a low voice. "Lighten your load and follow on."

Exiting the tree line out onto Marye's Heights with little discernable before them save the vague outline of a stacked rock wall, Joe commenced placing the men quickly, dispersing them in an old long traveled sunken road along the wall, while Daniel, mounted, tried in vain to peer through the fog laden valley before them.

Wash, running with an uneven gate, made his way hastily down a narrow path, blood soaking through the leg of his woolen pants. Hearing first, then reaching the bank of a shallow creek, he stopped and lifted his pants leg to reveal a deep gash in his left calf. He washed it quickly, splashing frigid water into the wound, working his finger into the puncture as far as he could bear, then, ripping a length of cloth from his shirt tail, wrapped and knotted it hastily around the wound. Taking his bearings, he struck off once again at a trot.

With the sounds of drums rolling upward from the valley, the fog began to lift, revealing long ranks of Union soldiers aligned at the edge of the town, moving forward deliberately in line of battle, each regiment led by its banner, hanging limp with the morning dew.

Behind the wall the Grays remained silent, watching intently the ominous waves of blue enemy, seemingly limitless in number and resolve. Daniel, trotted up and down the line behind them, assessing the situation.

"Grays! Make sure you are capped. No man fires until I give the command!"

"You heard the Cap'n!" yelled Sergeant McGee, moving quickly along the line, checking their spacing. "Hold your fire 'til ordered!"

Looking left and right, Daniel could see the lines of their Regiment extending far off in the distance.

Elsewhere, a double column of blue clad cavalry loped up a road, the hooves of their mounts slinging clods of moist earth as they passed. As the clanking of their swords and carbines faded away, Wash popped his head up from behind a large rotted log alongside of the road. Satisfied they were gone, he checked the bloody bandage on his leg, then regained the road, resuming his flight southward.

As the Union line, flags held high, made its way up the open plain toward the Grays, the Confederate batteries commenced firing sporadically from the heights behind, sending random shots in and among the advancing army. Daniel, dismounted, stood near Joe, both grimly judging the enemy's distance and rate of advance, when an ordinance sergeant trotted up and halted momentarily with a salute.

"How many rifles sir?"

"Seventy-three."

"You shall be resupplied with ammunition as required, sir," said the sergeant trotting off down the line.

A resounding *huzzah* was heard from down below as the drums changed their cadence, the Union lines breaking into double time.

"Hold steady men! Hold steady!" yelled Daniel.

The blue waves of soldiers were about two hundred yards away and closing as Daniel raised his sword.

"Ready..."

The clicking sounds of Enfields being brought to full cock were heard all along the wall as the enemy pulled to within a hundred yards.

"Fire!" he yelled dropping his sword.

The Columbia Grays' rifles erupted up and down the line, as did those of the adjacent companies, belching fire and pungent white smoke, setting small patches of grass before them to smolder with glowing bits of unspent powder. Hundreds of Union soldiers reeled and fell as the line faltered momentarily, then rallied and pressed on.

TRUE GRAY

"At will!" commanded Daniel. "Fire at will!"

Toward mid-afternoon Wash, dizzy with thirst, cautiously approached an unattended well, keeping a wary eye in all directions. Lowering the oaken bucket with a splash, he quickly cranked the handle and, retrieving the bucket, drank directly from it hurriedly, water dampening his chin and the front of his coat. Struck with the sudden sensation that he was being watched, he turned to see a young red-headed boy of about five, standing by the barn, holding a pale, staring, transfixed. Wash smiled, silently nodded thanks, then trotted off.

With a lull in the battle, Sergeant McGee and Corporal Whiting moved, crouching with a wooden box, distributing cartridges hastily, stepping over and around the dead and dying along the wall and in the sunken road while Daniel and Joe as well as Mabry, having picked up rifles, moved to fill gaps in the defense. As the smoke began to waft up and off to southward, the scene revealed before them proved horrific, with thousands of Union soldiers down on the field, most lying dead still while others cried for help or tried to pull themselves back along the ground. As the Grays feverishly reloaded, preparing for another assault, a lone Union sergeant broke from their retreating lines and sprinted forward, leaping over the bodies of his comrades toward a fallen banner. Sergeant McGee stopped his task momentarily to peer over the wall.

"Well, will you look at that bloke? Full of starch he is."

As he reached the flag and raised it, a Confederate sniper's shot rang out from somewhere down the wall, hitting the Yankee in the thigh. Reeling, he regained his feet and lifted the banner once more, defiantly.

"Jesus," yelled Sergeant McGee, straining to get a good look. "It's me brother in law!"

Dropping his end of the cartridge box, he vaulted over the wall and ran forward.

"Paddy! Come back!" yelled Daniel, jumping over the wall as well, sprinting after him. Another huge *huzzah* erupted from the enemy lines then as rallied, they surged forward for another attack. In answer the Confederate artillery bore down with a vengeance, blasting holes in the advancing ranks as the crack of Enfield rifle fire blazed away all up and down the wall.

TRUE GRAY

Close to midnight, a lone picket posted far out along the left flank of the Confederate position, perked up at the rustle of leaves somewhere off in the woods.

"Halt!" he called, cocking his rifle. "Who goes there?"

"A loyal Confederate!"

"What outfit?"

"Columbia Grays," returned the voice.

A horned owl hooted, then flushed silently into the night casting a fleeting moon shadow across the clearing separating the two.

"Who commanding?" inquired the picket.

"Marse... Cap'n Ledlow."

The picket pondered this for bit, then lowered his rifle hammer to half cock.

"You come on in then, with your hands up. Any funny stuff, I'll shoot you certain."

Wash limped out of the woods and into the moonlight, hands raised above his head, pant leg coated in dried blood, his blue Union coat turned inside out. The picket, a private from "A" Company, eyed Wash with circumspection, then motioned him to follow as he escorted him back through the Confederate lines.

"How the hell came you to be out there, friend?"

"Was made a prisoner 'while back, but I escaped. Been on the run since last night."

"You must be dog tired... and hungry," said the picket, handing him a johnny-cake from his haversack, which Wash began to devour as they walked on. "You was wrong about the Grays though. Captain Ledlow ain't in command no more. It's Lieutenant Fletcher."

The Columbia Grays slept in place along the wall, wrapped in dirty blankets against the cold, while every fourth man stood guard. With the dead and wounded having been carried from the road to be sorted out behind the lines, Joe sat with his back against a large rock in the wall, examining the company roster by lantern light. Despite the cover of their position they had taken nineteen casualties, almost a fourth of the Grays. He could only guess at what the rest of the regiment had sustained during the onslaught. Pulled from his thoughts, he glanced up to see Corporal Whiting approaching from down the sunken road, a soldier in tow, stepping over and around the bodies of the sleeping soldiers. Coming up at a crouch, just within the circle of lamplight, he halted with a salute.

"Look who's back sir."

Before Wash could salute, Joe was up and giving him an embrace.

"Wash! Where the hell have you been?"

"Captured, Marse Joe."

"Well thank God you made it back. We need you now more than ever. We still have your rifle," said Joe taking in the dreamlike vision of Wash's miraculous reappearance. Looking him over, he couldn't help but notice the dried blood encrusting his pant leg.

"Where's Marse Dan'l suh?"

"Out there, somewhere," said Joe sadly, motioning to the vast darkness of the field before them.

"Killed?"

"Almost certainly. A flea couldn't have survived out there. I'm sorry."

Wash stepped up to the wall and peered over into the darkness.

"Marse Joe. I got to go fetch him."

"No Wash. It's way too risky. Snipers from both sides are scanning the field for the least signs of advance. You'll be shot sure."

"Please Marse Joe. Please."

Joe studied Wash's grief-stricken face in the low lantern light, then opening his jacket with a sigh, drew his Griswold and Gunnison revolver.

"Here," he said handing it to Wash butt first. "Take this. And the lantern."

As Wash took the revolver and stuck it in his waist band, Joe turned to Corporal Whiting.

"Find him a full canteen... and a proper jacket."

"Thank you suh," said Wash.

Wash made his way out onto the field, the lantern turned low, trying as much as possible to walk clear of the bodies by moon light. Fifty yards out, he began to have difficulty maintaining his footing for the masses of the dead, an occasional moan exuding from the heaps of mutilated humanity. A phantom voice sounded eerily from some distance away.

"Please... please friend. Could you spare a pour soul a drink of water?"

Wash worked his way toward the voice, locating a Union soldier lying motionless on his side. Lifting the lantern slightly, he gently rolled him on his back to give him a drink, only to have

155

his entrails spill out, despite the poor wretch's attempts to hold them in. With a twitch, the disemboweled soldier fainted. As Wash turned away to resume his search, a sniper's bullet clipped the ground nearby smacking with a sickening thud into a dead body. Jumping reflexively, he tripped over a corpse, nearly extinguishing the lantern, his free hand landing in some cool goo that had once been a man's face. Scrambling to his knees and coaxing the lantern back to life, he saw on the ground before him a Confederate slouch hat with a palmetto cockade. Beside it lay a body, twisted in an awkward position, headless. Feverishly, Wash lifted the lantern to reveal the stripes of a Confederate First Sergeant on the sleeve.

"Shoot me," said a voice, as if in a trance, from somewhere to Wash's left. Turning quickly, Wash moved toward the utterance, fanning the lantern back and forth, catching at length the reflection of a familiar visage. It was Daniel, lying, his head leaned up against a dead Union soldier, eyes glazed over, unflinching in the lantern light. Wash dropped to his knees beside him.

"Marse Dan'l. It's Wash."

Daniel returned the same unknowing stare. Wash moved the lantern over his body, his gray woolen coat drenched in blood.

"I'm a redcoat... shoot me."

A drowsy guard for the Grays, hearing footsteps rapidly approaching, came to life and cocked his rifle.

"Hold your fire," ordered Joe.

Several sleeping soldiers awakened as Wash came into view, carrying Daniel on his back. With the guard covering, Joe and Corporal Whiting mounted the wall to help lift Daniel over, laying him gently on his back, as Wash followed, breathing heavily, covered in Daniel's blood. Joe leaned over him and listened as a group gathered around. To his astonishment, Daniel, though unconscious, was still alive.

CHAPTER SEVENTEEN

Three lanterns hung from tent poles, sending a pale sickly light over a blood-soaked, wood plank operating table. Major Pruitt, the sole surgeon for the Palmetto Regiment, wiped his hands off with a crimson stained, muslin rag as Private O'Conner handed him a cup of coffee.

"What time is it, Sean?"

"Comin' up on three in the mornin', sir."

Major Pruitt took a drink of the bitter, tepid coffee, drops of the umber colored liquid dripping from his huge moustache onto his blood smeared leather apron.

"We can't very well stop now, can we my boy?"

"No sir."

"Very well then," he said with a weary look. "Next!"

Wash and three other soldiers carried Daniel's limp form in and laid him on the table. The Major, noticing the captain's insignia on the collar, handed off his cup and pitched back in, making quick work of his examination, feeling of Daniel's carotid artery, lifting his eyelids to check his pupils as the surgeon's attendant, Corporal

Stedham, using a large nickel-plated pair of shears, cut the blood-soaked gray coat away.

"Forgive me..." muttered Daniel, coming to partially, as they maneuvered him to free the remainder of the coat. As Stedham then proceeded to cut away the vest, a solid object dropped out onto the table.

"Look at this sir," he said, picking up the small thick bible, turning it over in his hands, a distorted minie ball having firmly imbedded itself three fourths of the way through. Major Pruitt, preoccupied, cut away what remained of Daniel's cotton shirt and examined his torso. A ragged tear in his left side seeped blood while a coursing bullet wound creased his chest diagonally from left shoulder to right hip. His right arm, ripped by shrapnel, lay askew, the fractured bone jutting out just above the elbow. The surgeon checked the chest crease then daubed the wound at Daniel's side, assessing the extent of the damage.

"Nothing vital here, but this," he said motioning to the arm, "of course must go."

Corporal Stedham reached for the tourniquet, as Private O'Conner moved to stabilize Daniel's arm.

"No suh," said Wash stepping forward from the shadows.

"I beg your pardon?" said Major Pruitt, startled.

"You can't be cuttin' off his arm, suh. He's my master."

Pruitt looked at Wash, gravely.

"He will die if we do not. I assure you."

"You can't be cuttin' him up, suh. I... I won't allow it."

The surgeon, taken off guard, exchanged looks with Corporal Stedham.

"Wash?" sounded a weakened voice from the operating table.

"Yes, Marse Dan'l," said Wash stepping up alongside him. "I'm here."

"It's okay..."

Wash watched as Daniel drifted back into semi-consciousness, then, with a look of pained resignation, left the tent.

"Catlin knife," said Major Pruitt.

Wash walked out into the night, a half-moon intermittently appearing through the dark drifting clouds, while within the surgical tent Corporal Stedham dripped chloroform slowly from a glass vial onto a rag placed over Daniel's face. In moments, with Private O'Conner supporting Daniel's arm, Major Pruitt calmly made a deft cut all the way around above the elbow with the long, cold, freshly wiped blade. Exhausted, Wash slumped to the ground, drained, forsaken as the surgeon, manipulating a scalpel, cut through muscle, tendon and connective tissue, Daniel's body twitching involuntarily at the affront. From without the tent then came the low mournful sounds of Wash's baritone voice.

"We are, climbing, Jacob's Ladder..."

Major Pruitt handed Stedham the scalpel and wiped his face with his sleeve as blood poured into a pan O'Conner held beneath the horrifically traumatized appendage.

"We are, climbing, Jacob's Ladder..." continued Wash, sitting, rocking in anguish.

As Corporal Stedham pulled back on the severed flesh above the cut on Daniel's arm exposing the blood smeared whiteness of living humerus, the major plied the capital bone saw, releasing the sickly smell of drilled teeth, of burnt horn.

"We are, climbing, Jacob's ladder..."

TRUE GRAY

Daniel's arm came loose into Private O'Conner's hands as he turned routinely and carried it out back to the limb pile.

"Soldiers... of the... cross..."

Wash, head down, heaved in sorrow.

CHAPTER EIGHTEEN

An open hospital bay in Richmond with thirty beds on either side, having been recently scrubbed and whitewashed throughout, glowed in the morning light as several nurses followed Captain Dubois on his rounds, the combined smell of camphor, alcohol and burning wood from two centrally located potbelly stoves permeating the air. Another nurse sponged cool water on Daniel's feverish face and neck as Wash, sitting against the wall by his bed looked on. Daniel had been sleeping fitfully, uncomfortably for two days. As Captain Dubois approached, Wash rose to his feet. Taking Daniel's wrist in hand and pulling a silver watch from his vest pocket, the captain studied the second hand carefully. With a grim look, he released Daniel's wrist, felt of his forehead, spoke a few words in a low voice to the nurse and continued on.

"Miss... how is he?" asked Wash.

"Dangerously close to succumbing to an infection I'm afraid," said the nurse, resuming her sponging.

"What can we do?"

Daniel heaved an involuntary sigh, unconscious, his face flush and turgid.

"If the fever doesn't break soon," she said, daubing cool water gently along his hairline, "Captain Dubois will be forced to re-amputate."

In a nearby woods, Wash walked, crunching through dry leaves, listening for the sound of water ahead, the day bracingly chill, despite the breaking of the sun through wintery clouds. Reaching Shokoe creek, he followed along the bank, then finding a calm pocket with back eddies, leaned forward, peering into the muddy recesses of the sedimented bottom.

Within the boiled whiteness of the sheeted bed, Daniel lay, delirious, fresh beads of perspiration forming on his forehead.

Alongside a small, stunted, darkish barked shrub, Wash knelt and examined the last remaining tear drop shaped leaves, picking several and turning them in his fingers.

The nurse, trying in vain to get Daniel to drink, held a glass beaker with a thin steel nozzle to his lips. Coughing involuntarily, he turned his head.

Walking slowly through a stand of willow trees, Wash spotted high among the branches an abandoned bird's nest, then hunching forward with his hands on his knees, thoroughly scoured the ground beneath.

The following morning found Wash curled up in a gray woolen blanket, sound asleep on the floor beside Daniel's bed. Captain Dubois, leaning over holding a stethoscope to Daniel's chest, listened carefully, then raised up.

"It would appear as if we have had a turn for the better," he said to the nurse, in a low voice. "Freshen his bed clothes please."

"Yes sir," she said, as the captain continued quietly on down the ward. With the captain gone, she felt of Daniel's forehead, touching lightly with her fingers. Indeed, it would seem that his fever had broken somewhat. Lighthearted then at the rare success in their otherwise discouraging endeavors, she commenced to gently turn down Daniel's sheet. As she made her way toward the foot of the bed, gathering the cloth, she suddenly stopped, stepping back, alarmed. A bundle of some sort was tied to Daniel's right foot, consisting of what appeared to be a small turtle shell stuffed with dark thread like plant roots and tiny striated bird feathers. Catching her breath, she looked toward Wash, still asleep in his blanket on the floor.

The streets of Richmond were covered in a light, February snow as Wash, a cloth bundle tucked beneath his arm, made his way happily along a narrow alley. Turning onto Capitol Street, he veered into the frozen, rutted earth of the roadway, clear of the few shoppers and pedestrians who walked along the boardwalks. As he picked up his pace westward, loaded wagons of dry goods, tied hay, cord wood, and fodder creaked past, interspersed by the occasional buggy or rider on horseback, braving the bracing morning air, while blasts of white breath puffed from the flaring nostrils of the horses and mules.

Sitting up in his hospital bed, Daniel, with what remained of his right arm wrapped in a clean white bandage, smiled as a pretty young volunteer handed him a white stoneware cup of hot black coffee from a pewter tray.

"Thank you, Hannah," he said gripping the cup awkwardly with his left hand.

She smiled shyly and continued her rounds while, from the end of the bay, entered Wash, stopping momentarily to warm his hands on one of the wood stoves before making his way to Daniel's bed.

"Must be pretty blustery out there. You look chilled."

Wash placed the cloth bundle in Daniel's lap, smiling.

"Been a foragin', Marse Dan'l. Apple turnovers."

"Well now, you don't say. Pull up a chair then and help me. We must dispatch them swiftly before the ward authorities find us out."

Sitting close by, Wash unwrapped the delectable treasures and held them forth, taking Daniel's coffee cup to allow him to select one.

"Be sure to extend my compliments to the baker," said Daniel, savoring the sweet cinnamon dusted apple, baked and tucked in brown crispy crust, drizzled with sugar glaze.

"I would," said Wash, munching away, "but then she'd figure out some was missin'. How're you feelin' today?"

"Okay. Except for the strange pains that come and go now and then... in the arm I no longer have."

"When do they aim to send you back home?"

Daniel looked thoughtfully at the half pastry still in his hand.

"I've decided to keep up the fight. I'm not going home."

"But Marse Dan'l..."

"I'm not ready for them to see me like this, Wash. I would rather stay on and try to beat these people back. Besides, I just wave a sword around and yell anyway. I can still manage that."

Wash considered this as he finished his turnover. Seeing that Daniel had taken his last bite as well, he whisked away the evidential crumbs into the cloth and folded it up into his jacket pocket.

"I would like for you to find a sheet of paper and pen. I must dictate something to you. My left handwriting is atrocious."

"Okay, Marse Dan'l. A letter?"

"No," said Daniel. "A statement of intent. I am freeing you."

Wash stared back at Daniel, then lowered his gaze, struck with a rush of conflicting emotions. Daniel watched as Wash seemed to consider his hands, resting on his knees. Turning them palms up, he folded them together into his chest.

"No man can really own another one in the eyes o' the Lord," he said.

A few drops, like spatters of light rain, dampened the front of his gray woolen jacket.

"I've always known I was free... in my heart."

Daniel studied him closely as Hannah, passing back through the bay, paused momentarily at the foot of the bed, then moved on unnoticed. Wash wiped his eyes with his sleeve and rose to his feet.

"Well, if I'm a free man under the law, I can do whatever I want now. Right?"

"Yes Wash. That's right."

"Well then... I'm stayin' too, Marse Dan'l. If'n it's alright with you."

Daniel, moved, extended a left handshake. As Wash grasped it, Daniel pulled him to, in a one-armed bear hug.

169

CHAPTER NINETEEN

On the deeply rutted road leading westward out of Richmond rode Daniel with Wash by his side, astride borrowed mounts, Daniel's new jean wool shell jacket pinned neatly up at the sleeve. Tending a garden near the road, a thin, flaxen haired woman, aged well beyond her years, stood up to rub her back, holding a hand full of freshly dug parsnips. As they walked their horses past, she gazed over the cross laid, split rail fence bordering her plot, studied the one armed officer and his colored companion for a moment, then bent back to her meager harvest.

Days later, sitting on a stump in an encampment near Lynchburg, Joe Fletcher busied himself shaving in a polished steel mirror hung on a pitch pine, a straight razor in one hand, a battered tin cup of soapy water in the other. Nearby Mabry, leaning over a fire, slid chopped wild greens and onions off of a well-worn cutting board with a camp knife into a stew pot. A lone Rebel yell suddenly broke the silence from somewhere east of camp. Joe dropped his razor in his soap cup and stood, looking in the direction of the call, while Mabry, replacing the pot lid and setting the board aside, did likewise. Another yell was heard then, followed by a *hurrah* as the commotion drew nearer. Wiping his face hastily with a rag, Joe exchanged looks with Mabry as the two of them headed off toward the source of the excitement. Within fifty yards, through the makeshift tents, the campfires, the stacks of rifles, bedrolls and haversacks, they were met by an impromptu parade of ragged Columbia Grays, surrounding Daniel and Wash, clamoring at the sides of their mounts, overjoyed at the reappearance of their commander and the man responsible for his deliverance.

May of 1864 found the Grays encamped near Spotsylvania, they having managed to survive a scrape along the Rapidan followed by a harsh winter, hungrier and leaner than before, but with an unbroken will. While Wash busied himself repairing a bridle with a pocket knife and a strip of rawhide, Daniel, seated against a tree studying a tattered map, was pulled from his thoughts by the footsteps of Corporal, turned Sergeant, Whiting, making his way at a quick walk through camp toward them.

"Sir, we have a rather interesting target of opportunity up front," he said saluting. "I should think Wash could be of some service, sir?"

"Oh?" said Daniel, laying his map down on his lap. "What type of target?"

"An officer sir. Exposing himself rather recklessly. Fairly high ranking I believe."

Daniel looked toward Wash, who returned a willing smile. Daniel nodded as Wash dropped what he was doing, secured his rifle and ammunition pouch, and headed out with Sergeant Whiting at a trot.

Near the edge of a thick stand of poplars crouched two Confederates, taking cover amid the shadows. Before them lay a long expanse of undulating fields planted in barley and tobacco. As they glassed the enemy, Sergeant Whiting and Wash came trotting up, slowing to a walk, then dropping to a crawl as they came alongside.

"Looks to be a General maybe," said the one who seemed to be in charge of the reconnaissance, handing the telescope to Whiting. Sergeant Whiting took a quick look down range, then passed the glass to Wash.

At Spindle Farm, a Union major general, replete in his magnificent blue broadcloth coat adorned with double starred epaulettes and a triple row of brass buttons, uncharacteristically directed the placement of artillery. While junior officers scrambled about to relay instructions, field pieces were being moved hastily about with the aid of mules and men.

"How far?" asked Wash, having located the animated officer in the telescope.

"We have it at about six hundred," said the other Confederate.

Wash passed the glass to him and commenced to adjust the rear sight on his Enfield, while the two looked askance at Sergeant Whiting, he returning a nod of affirmation.

"Here," said the leader, handing Wash his rifle. "use the Whitworth."

Wash took it in hand, eyeing it for a moment, then checking the sights and cap, assumed a kneeling position resting the piece within the low crotch of a tree.

Back at Spindle Farm the general fumed and gesticulated, irritated at the timidity of his artillerists who had become unnerved by the occasional sniper fire which had troubled them periodically since sunrise. Doubling back across the line of cannon, followed closely by his adjutant, he nudged a young soldier with his boot who had been hunkering down behind a limber.

"Get up young man and do your duty. There is no sense in dodging about. They couldn't hit an elephant at this distance."

As the shamed soldier gathered his courage and prepared to stand, a whistling sound was heard, followed by a sickening slap as the general turned to his adjutant, a neat hole having appeared beneath his left eye. Swaying momentarily as a small, crimson, streamlet began to course down his face, he fell into the adjutant's arms, dead.

The following morning found the Columbia Grays positioned behind a split rail fence, busily digging themselves in. As two soldiers jabbed at the ground with bayonets in an effort to excavate a low place, another nearby scraped soil and rocks with a tin pan, dumping it at the base of the fence to form a berm in front of him, patting it down hastily with his hands. Wash and Mabry having located a dead tree trunk, dragged it into position at the base of the fence, Wash, eyeing the roots for possible rifle rests as Mabry tamped dirt around the base to hold it in position. Moving along the line, Sergeant Whiting checked the progress, encouraging the men to keep to their preparations.

By mid-afternoon the battle appeared to be drawing near as Daniel, with Joe by his side, glassed the enemy lines at Spindle Farm. The Union forces, fully equipped and amassed in force, stretched as far as he could see to the left and right, clearly outnumbering anything the south had in place.

"Bring the men to the ready," said Daniel handing the telescope to Joe. "This appears to be big."

"To the ready," said Joe to Sergeant Whiting, collapsing the telescope and returning it to its case.

"To the ready!" yelled Sergeant Whiting several times in succession as he paced their defensive position, the men relaying the command up and down the line. "Check your charges boys. This looks to be a ground hog case. We're not budging from here."

To their forefront a blue clad officer, in full parade uniform, commenced galloping up and down the Union line, waving his hat as the northern troops set up a rolling cheer. Completing his circuit and returning to his position, the field fell into a deathly silence as the Grays watched and waited. Wash glanced back at Daniel who stood behind the line, grimly focused on the enemy. Suddenly, without warning a row of white smoke dots appeared along the high ground behind the enemy.

"Take cover!" yelled Daniel as cannon shells careened in with fury, skipping along the ground, falling into the woods behind them, blasting the trees to bits. A shell hit the Gray's line, taking out a swatch of split rails and three Confederates with it, another exploding twenty feet to their front, throwing dirt and rocks over all the soldiers in its path while the Grays hugged the earth for all they were worth. Scarcely a minute later the cannonade ceased as abruptly as it had begun, followed by a ghostly quiet as the acrid smoke drifted gently off toward the northwest. As the view of the field began to clear, a lone bugle call was heard, followed by the sounds of drums.

"We will hold them as far back, for as long as possible," yelled Daniel, raising his arm. Any man who thinks he can hit his mark may do so at will. Make every shot count. Give them a good taste of the Grays!"

With the long blue lines still three hundred yards away and closing, a shot rang out, as a Union color bearer fell back, clinging to his banner. Wash hastily reloaded as the sporadic crack of Enfields commenced up and down the line. At this, the northern soldiers broke into quick time as the firing along the fence increased in intensity. Mabry, holding steady, fired his rifle with a cracking recoil and blast of black powder.

"Give it to 'em, boys!" yelled Joe, pacing behind the rifle line. "Fire... fire!" At this, he spun and fell, a minie ball having hit him in the side. With the Union attack scarcely two hundred yards out Wash took careful aim again and fired, dropping another soldier, then quickly pulled out another paper cartridge.

"Here Wash!" said Private Ephraim Henderson to his left, trading rifles with him. Wash took aim and fired and was handed another rifle from Private Willie Shaw on his right. He fired again only to be handed another loaded rifle from Henderson.

"Give 'em holy hell, Wash!" Yelled Ephraim. "You shoot, we'll reload!"

CHAPTER TWENTY

Two Days before Christmas, chilled and battle weary but glad to be clear of campaign season, the Grays camped amid a stand of bare yellow birch along the James River, feeding a series of fires in an effort to stay warm. Daniel, sitting before one of the fires on a makeshift split log bench, wrapped in a ragged wool blanket, sipped steaming barley juice, their coffee supply having long since succumbed to the blockade, and stared into the flames. With his mind several hundred miles away, he was brought back to the present by the appearance of Joe, a captured great coat thrown over his shoulders, hobbling up to take a seat beside him, leaning toward the fire to warm his hands.

"How's the hip?"

"Coming along."

"Doesn't look like it."

"Well, with the cold weather and all..."

"Joe," said Daniel with a sigh. "I'm afraid I must issue you an order. You are my subordinate, are you not?"

Joe gave a look of acquiescence.

"Then I order you home, as soon as you are able."

"But..."

"To wholly recuperate. We will need you desperately come early spring."

Joe gazed into the fire, thinking, as Daniel tossed off the meager concoction and thought of home.

"There is something else," said Daniel, setting his cup down and gathering his blanket about his neck. There is a young woman in Columbia. Miss Megan Hale. You know of her perhaps?"

"The Belle of Gervais. Of course." Joe added a chunk of split wood to the fire, sending red sparkles spiraling upward into the night.

"I doubt she still waits for me. But just in case she does... you must dissuade her. I am no longer worthy. A woman like her... she deserves a complete man. Make her to understand, Joe. Please."

Joe glanced at Daniel, who sat staring into the crackling fire, clasping the blanket about his neck with his one hand.

"Yes Daniel. Yes sir."

A slight commotion was heard as Daniel turned to see Wash and Mabry making their way through camp, lugging a load between them, wrapped in a dirty tarp.

"Ah, our accomplished foragers. And how did we fare this evening?"

Wash and Mabry dropped the tarp by the light of the fire.

"Not bad, Marse Dan'l," replied Wash. "Four chickens, a half bushel o' ear corn..."

Mabry flipped open the tarp triumphantly.

"... and a keg o' whiskey," added Mabry, grinning.

"Merry Christmas Marse Dan'l!" beamed Wash.

"Merry Christmas indeed," said Daniel. "Tell all who wish to partake to bring their cup."

"Yes suh," replied Wash, as Mabry trotted off into the darkness, eager to spread the word.

By midnight the entire air of the encampment had transformed itself, as soldiers gathered around the south end of camp to clap and slap their knees in time to Sergeant Whiting claw-hammering "Soldier's Joy" on his tack head banjo. Close by, Mabry accompanied him on bones while

Private Willie Shaw, standing upon a stump, tapped his bare foot and puffed out a bass rhythm on a stoneware jug. Among the crowd assembled sat Private Ephraim Henderson on a wagon tongue, sipping from his tin cup and grinning.

Back by the command campfire, Daniel and Wash relaxed, savoring the smoky taste of the gift whiskey of unknown origin and listening from a distance to the camp music which was steadily building in enthusiasm. Wash pulled a glowing stick from the fire and lit his corncob pipe, puffing it to life.

"What you plannin' on doin' with yourself when this whole flap blows over, Marse Dan'l?"

"Guess I'll head on back home and help Father pick up the pieces. Get the plantation back up and running. If there is anything left of it. And you?"

"Me?" said Wash looking up at the quarter moon just beginning to cloud over. "Well don't laugh now. But if we was to make it back all safe and sound, I plan on findin' me a girl to marry, and a plot of land to work. Build a tight little cabin and raise greens and corn. And maybe get some chickens and a pig or two. And have some children and show 'em how to read and write and do their times tables... and take 'em down to Robber's Hole so's I could teach 'em to swim."

Daniel gazed into the fire, lost momentarily in the picture Wash had painted.

"I can help with the land, Wash."

"Oh, I would work real hard and pay it off in no time Marse Dan'l. You'd see."

"No. It would be yours free and clear," said Daniel. "You saved me. I would have died out there on the field. Nothing I can do now could ever..."

The sound of Sergeant Whiting's banjo, kicking into rhythm, was accompanied by a raucous Rebel yell.

"Wash!... Wash!... come sing!" yelled Ephraim Henderson from off in the darkness, joined by a chorus of others.

"You'll have to find your own girl though," said Daniel as Wash rose to oblige the revelers. "I've got no standing in that area."

At the south end of camp where the last of the barrel whiskey had found its home, the party was in full swing, Whiting's driving banjo accompanied by Mabry on bones as well as the claps, foot stomps and whoops of the crowd of heartened Grays. Willie Shaw, doing his best to clog atop a stump, was shoved off by Private Ben

TRUE GRAY

Parker who promptly mounted the stump in an attempt to cut a pigeon wing. As Wash approached, Ben made a fatal misstep, landing on his butt with a thud and a groan, to the great amusement of his comrades. Ephraim then, loath to demure in a crisis, hopped upon the stump and, on wobbly legs, attempted a proper quadrille as Wash commenced to sing.

> *Oh, I wish I was in the land of cotton,*
> *Old times there are not forgotten,*
> *Look away, look away, look away Dixieland.*
>
> *In Dixie's land where I was born,*
> *Early on one frosty mornin',*
> *Look away, look away, look away Dixieland.*

Ephraim, having succumbed to a case of tanglefoot, was dragged off the stump and replaced by Mabry who, still playing the bones, commenced a rhythmic shuffling of his feet in time to the music.

> *I wish I was in Dixie, Hooray, hooray!*
> *In Dixie's land I'll make my stand,*
> *To live and die in Dixie.*
> *Away, away, away down south in Dixie.*
> *Away, away, away down south in Dixie.*

TRUE GRAY

Dawn found the Gray's encampment silent, covered in new snow, soldier's laying here and there among and around smoldering fires, curled up in dingy, snow flocked blankets or thread bare coats, sleeping it off. Wash flipped a tarp off of his face and yawned, looking about and blinking at the orange tinted whiteness of the scene. Crawling out of his makeshift bedding, he made his way, shivering, stepping around the whiskey casualties, toward the command fire. With an iron poker, he probed about the dormant fire, exposing some live coals still smoldering beneath the ashes. Breaking a handful of sticks and placing the bundle upon the coals, he dropped to his hands and knees and began to blow softly.

Back in the woods, barely visible through the icy fog of morning, appeared the faint outline of human forms. As Wash continued to puff gently, gradually coaxing the fire back to life, the line of forms silently approached, a rank of malevolent ghosts pressing forward through the dim morning light. With his efforts beginning to pay off, a small flame popped up through the sticks. As Wash reached for more kindling to add, the figures, silhouetted in the cold misty dawn, appeared to halt as if dressing their line. Encouraged by his success, Wash reached out his numb fingers to warm them over the burgeoning flames.

"Charge!" yelled a harsh voice from close by as a rush of attackers poured through the woods, yelling like demons. Wash scrambled for cover as his groggy comrades awakened with a start, alarmed, disoriented, hung over. As the raiders reached the encampment, bent on destruction, they commenced pelting the Grays relentlessly with snowballs.

"Caught 'em nappin' boys," yelled Sergeant Hawes of Company "A". "No whiskey for us, no mercy for them. Get 'em!"

"This'll teach 'em some manners by God!" yelled another attacker in the act of flinging a snowball.

Daniel, emerging in a rush from his tent, buttoning his pants, was immediately pelted in the chest with a particularly well delivered projectile which exploded in a blast of white powder.

"Rally! Rally Grays! Sergeant Whiting! Form the counter attack!" yelled Daniel.

CHAPTER TWENTY-ONE
(April 1865)

Sergeant Whiting walked briskly through camp, the woods near Boon Hill, North Carolina alive with all things blooming, past soldiers cleaning their rifles, others repairing what remained of their ragged uniforms. Private Ephraim Henderson sat on a log, shirtless, sewing on hand whittled, elm wood buttons to replace those missing on his tattered shirt, his snow-white body spare and rangy, his ribs showing through. Further on Private Ben Parker, seated on the ground, worked with a pen knife on a stubborn thorn imbedded in the sole of his leathery bare foot, while near him Private Willie Shaw tried out a freshly plaited grass hat band, fitting it over his bullet riddled, brown felt slouch.

At the far end of the encampment, Wash, using a stump for a butcher's block, worked at skinning a rabbit he had managed to snare while Daniel, seated on the ground against a hickory, perused a newly delivered dispatch. Wash stopped his work at the sound of Sergeant Whiting's approach and watched curiously as he halted before Daniel with a salute.

"You sent for me Captain?"

"Yes," said Daniel, folding the dispatch one handed and tucking it away in his inside jacket pocket. "We will be reconnoitering a ford to our west. Choose three men and have them ready in ten minutes."

"Yes sir," said Whiting, saluting, then turning on his heels to hurry off. Wash, suspending his work, poured water over his hands from a jug and wiped them quickly on his pants.

Proceeding single file, Daniel and Wash accompanied by Privates Henderson, Shaw and Parker, made their way stealthily through the underbrush of a thick forest, stopping frequently to listen. After some time, Daniel, raising his hand, called for a halt and kneeled, pulling his map from his jacket pocket while the men crouched to wait. As he worked to spread out the map, Wash lent a hand, holding the other end as Daniel studied it momentarily, then nodded to the group, indicating the direction. Silently, they arose and continued on, Wash tending to the map, putting it in order and passing it back to Daniel.

Making their way down a gentle slope in the woods, the far-off sound of water became barely audible in the distance. As they pressed on cautiously, the trees became progressively taller, the sound of the water gradually more pronounced. At length Daniel halted, peering through the woods at what would appear to be the sought-after ford in the river some hundred feet ahead, the light dancing off disturbances on the surface, as though rippling over a shoal of gravel or perhaps a plate of rock. Henderson and Shaw fanned out to the flanks instinctively, Parker guarding the rear, as Daniel motioned all forward for a better view. A lark in a nearby nest, commenced to warble, warning all who would listen, then dropped silent. Suddenly a *click,* was heard some distance off to the right front. Wash, alerting quickly to the sound, scanned, then caught a fleeting glimpse through a break in the trees of a blue jacketed figure, kneeling. As he dove in front of Daniel, the crack of the enemy rifle desecrated the silence of the forest, birds flushing in alarm from the trees above.

Henderson and Shaw moved instantly to the front, straining for a shot as the splashing of the sentry's boots were heard in rapid retreat across the ford. Daniel and Private Parker rushed to Wash who lay motionless, face down in the leaves.

Gently, they rolled him onto his back to find his eyes open but unfocused, a scarlet spot in the chest of his gray jacket, widening. With trembling hands, Parker unbuttoned Wash's jacket, then pulling out his knife, cut open his pullover shirt. A bullet hole in Wash's breast oozed the last of his life blood as Parker looked sadly up at Daniel.

Shaw and Henderson, having lost the trail of the enemy, returned winded, and looked on in shock to find Daniel, kneeling by Wash's side, giving witness to his slipping away. The woods stood silent, not a bird, breeze, rustle of leaves, nothing, save the soft distant ripple of the ford. While Daniel looked on, watching helplessly as Wash's eyes seemed to settle on him momentarily then glaze over, a thin leather lace strung about Wash's neck caught his eye. Lifting it gently over his head, Daniel rose to his feet to examine the treasure it secured, the palmetto button.

The men carried Wash's lifeless body slowly through the woods while Daniel followed, clutching the button in his hand. Proceeding out of the woods, and making their way across an open grassy field, a covey of quail scattered before them, unacknowledged by the bearers.

TRUE GRAY

The following morning rose on a dense fog laying heavily in and around the lowlands, leaving the tops of the blue green hills visible as if undiscovered islands in a desolate land, rising up from a vaporous sea. As the mist rolled, thick and liquid like below, a procession made its way slowly, deliberately, up a seldom traveled road, tracing a ridge toward a gently rounded promontory. In the lead rode Daniel, astride his gray, with Mabry driving the company wagon close behind. Twenty yards back marched what remained of the Columbia Grays, in columns of four, under the control of Sergeant Whiting. Four Artillerists from Fourth Battery, tending a bronze twelve-pounder pulled by six mules, brought up the rear.

At the summit two soldiers, finishing their work, climbed out of the grave and stood respectfully with their shovels. Circling the wagon, Mabry brought the team around and halted near the grave site, set the brake, and stepped down. Sergeant Whiting halted the column as they commence to close ranks.

"Right, face!" came the command from Whiting as they turned to face eastward.

As Daniel dismounted, passing his reins to Mabry, Sergeant Whiting, Parker, Henderson and

Shaw gently lifted Wash's body, sewn into his gray blanket, from the wagon bed and carried him, laying him softly on a worn tarpaulin spread upon the ground alongside the grave. Daniel, sword buckled on, took up a position at the foot while Whiting retrieved a cloth bundle from the wagon seat and, with the help of the pall bearers, unfolded it. Together they spread the tattered, Confederate battle flag over Wash, tucking the edges gently about him. Once satisfied, Sergeant Whiting turned toward the Grays, calling them to attention.

The sunrise, just beginning to spill over the hills in the distance poured forth, tinting the vapor sea in shades of orange and red.

"Present... Arms!" commanded Sergeant Whiting, the men shifting their battered rifles before them vertically, trigger forward, while Daniel saluted with his sword.

At this the cannon fired, rocking back in its carriage, cleaving the morning air, sending a ring of white smoke out over the lowlands before them, expanding, ethereal. With Whiting, Shaw, Parker and Henderson gripping the edges of the tarpaulin, they lowered Wash's body into the grave, while the soldiers in the ranks stood grief stricken, numbed by the loss.

"Order... Arms!" said Whiting as the last traces of powder from the cannon melded into the sunrise.

As shovels of black earth dropped upon the handstitched Saint Andrew's cross of Wash's shroud, the Grays and the cannoneers marched back down the road from whence they'd come, dejected, forlorn, behind Mabry in the wagon which, through the entire campaign, had never seemed so empty. Winding their way solemnly down the ridge, they disappeared at length in their descent towards camp. Beneath the rising sun which gained strength, lighting up the lowlands, driving the valley fog off and upward like battle haze, stood Daniel, alone at Wash's grave.

The soldiers watched silently as, toward afternoon, Daniel rode slowly back into camp. Reaching his empty command site, he halted, Mabry stepping up to hold the bridle as he dismounted. Nearby Sergeant Whiting stood, watching. Somewhere outside of camp the gradual sound of a loping horse was heard as Grays parted and directed the dispatch rider toward their Captain.

"Commander Company "C", sir?" said the horseman, coming to a halt and dismounting with a salute.

"Yes, Corporal," said Daniel returning the salute.

"Sir, I am here to inform you that General Lee has surrendered, sir, written orders to follow in short order."

"Surrendered?"

"Yes sir."

"As of when?"

"April ninth, sir. Day before yesterday, sir."

Daniel, standing mute, appeared not to have heard this, as the dispatch rider stood by awkwardly.

"By your leave, sir," he said, preparing to resume his mission. As Daniel stood unresponsive, Sergeant Whiting nodded, waving him onward. Saluting, the dispatch rider swung up into his saddle and trotted off.

Daniel, alone, walked aimlessly through the woods, the air deafeningly still, save the rustling of leaves and pine needles crunching beneath his boots. Glancing off of a tree trunk with his shoulder, then another, he staggered slightly, continuing on through the woods. A raven watched him from a branch high above as he picked up the pace, wild thorny vines scratching and snagging his war worn uniform. A broken branch caught the pinned-up sleeve of his coat, spinning him off balance momentarily. Regaining his footing, the earth beneath him reeling, Daniel drew his sword and attacked the vines, the brush, the trees, hacking away with rage, at anything and everything... the atmosphere, the light, the world, until at last exhausted he flung his sword away, leaning back against a tree, gasping for breath. Spent, he slid down to the ground, lost, beaten.

CHAPTER TWENTY-TWO

In an encampment near Durham, North Carolina, Privates Henderson and Shaw furled the colors of Company "C" for the last time as the Columbia Grays stacked their rifles in a pile, one at a time, and moved slowly away. Daniel, mounted, having addressed the men, saluted them in farewell, then reining his mount southward, rode away, the Grays looking on in silent regret. Three miles on he encountered an aged rock bridge, crossing over a stream of running water, before setting out upon a long, rutted road extending straight before him. Toward afternoon he overtook a group of Confederates headed for home, thin, ragged, barefoot. Further on he encountered three more resting on the side of the road, hollow eyed with fatigue and hunger, yet not too weak to stand and salute an officer passing by. Daniel returned the salute and rode on.

A week later near Cheraw, South Carolina, Daniel broke out of a heavy tree line and began winding his way down a sloping road, bathed in the morning sun, a broad panorama extending before him as far as he could see. Reaching the lowlands at length, he commenced walking the gray easily alongside a dry stacked rock wall, slowly approaching an aged woman in a work apron and bonnet, hands on her hips, taking him in. As Daniel neared, she lifted a stoppered gourd on a rope and handed it to him, her weathered knowing eyes signaling him homeward. Doffing his hat in thanks, he continued on, drinking the buttermilk as he rode.

Toward afternoon four days later, Daniel came upon a destroyed bridge, water bouncing around and over the broken rock pillars that once served as support. Clinging to the gray's mane, he swam the Wateree, emerging soaked but safely on the far bank. The next morning found him riding slowly through the largely abandoned streets of Columbia, charred and in ruins, still smoldering in places. A couple with three small children and a colored male servant, sifting through the rubble that was their home, stopped and stared as Daniel rode by.

Back at last upon a familiar country lane, Daniel rode past fields where negroes, still trying to work the unkempt rows, rose up and looked, questioningly. Exhausted from days on the road, he reined the gray at last into the entrance of the

Ledlow plantation, the iron gates rusting and sagging in disrepair.

Julia sat on the porch shelling peas when a faint clopping of hooves caused her to stop and rise, peering warily at the ragged, bearded, one armed stranger, making his way along the once pristinely cindered drive toward the house. As the rider approached, his mount raising its head, ears perked forward, she put down her basket and went quickly into the house. In short order, Sophia, Ruth and Sarah at Julia's beckoning hurried onto the porch, followed by Uncle Gabe and Aunt Nettie, while Bessie came running from the garden. Nathan, in shirtsleeves, followed closely by Toby, strode hastily from around the side of the house, stopping by the steps as the rider came to a halt.

"Daniel?... Is that you?" asked Nathan.

"It's all lost... Wash too. I wish it had been me."

They all went to him, helping him from his horse, hugging him in turns.

"I'm sorry," he said, receiving an embrace from Julia. "God, I am so sorry."

Together they escorted him up the steps and into the house.

TRUE GRAY

EPILOGUE

Crystal clear water spilled over the run into the pool of Robber's Hole while the dark, towering, cypress trees threw undulating shadows upon the tranquil surface, calm save the splash of an occasional perch after an insect. Finches chirped and flitted about the branches above as a squirrel fussed and chattered nearby, seemingly taking notice of a form moving mysteriously beneath the surface, white, obscured, rising. Suddenly, emerging from below, breached Daniel, gazing straight up into the sunlight splintering through the tree tops, the palmetto button strung securely about his neck.

TRUE GRAY

EXTRACTS

There are at the present moment, many colored men in the Confederate Army doing duty not only as cooks, servants, and laborers, but as real soldiers, having muskets on their shoulders and bullets in their pockets, ready to shoot down loyal troops and do all that soldiers may do to destroy the Federal government and build up that of the traitors and rebels.

Frederick Douglass, 1861

The war has dispelled one delusion of the abolitionists. The Negroes regard them as enemies instead of friends. No insurrection has occurred in the South—no important stampede of slaves has evinced their desire for freedom. On the contrary, they have jeered at and insulted our troops, have readily enlisted in the rebel army and on Sunday, at Manassas, shot down our men with as much alacrity as if abolitionism had never existed.

The Northern Exchange, 1861

TRUE GRAY

It is undoubtedly true that, notwithstanding the strenuous efforts of abolitionists, the Negroes bear the yoke cheerfully and heartily join their fortunes to those of their masters in the great struggle in which they are now engaged.

James Ferguson, Blackwood's
Magazine, England, 1862

Negroes as a mass have shown no friendship to the Union—have neither sought to achieve their liberty nor to subdue their masters... Their sympathies are with the rebels...The truth is that there never was a greater humbling than the talk about Negro loyalty. Abolition has asserted it from the beginning of the war, but every fact of the times proves it a mere assertion.

Providence Post, Rhode Island. 1862

At four o'clock this morning the rebel army began to move from our town, Jackson's force taking the Advance. The most liberal calculation could not have given them more than 64,000 men. Over 3,000 Negroes must be included in that number. These were clad in all kinds of uniforms, not only cast off or captured United States uniforms, but in coats with Southern buttons, State buttons, etc. They were shabby, but no shabbier or seedier than those worn by the white men in the rebel ranks. Most of the Negroes had arms, rifles, muskets, sabers, bowie knives, dirks, etc. They were supplied, in many instances, with knapsacks, haversacks, canteens, etc., and were manifestly an integral portion of the Southern Confederate Army. They were seen riding on horses and mules, driving wagons, riding on caissons, in ambulances, with the staff of Generals, and promiscuously mixed up with all the rebel horde.

Capt. Isaac W. Heysinger, Maryland, 1862

From what I have seen of the Southern Negroes, I am of the opinion that the Confederates could, if they chose, convert a great number into soldiers... I think that they would prove more efficient than black troops under any other circumstances.

Lt. Col. Arthur Fremantle, British Coldstream Guards, 1863

TRUE GRAY

Among the rebel prisoners who were marched through Gettysburg there were observed seven negroes in uniform and fully accoutered as soldiers.

New York Herald, July 24, 1863

We had a small chunk of a fight with the Lincolnit[es] the 2 day of this instant. We killed six of them & taken one prisoner & wounded ten more. Jack Thomas a colored person that belongs to our company killed one of them...

John N.T. Hammonds to "Dear Uncle," Feb. 10, 1862

You ask me to tell you all I know of my late dear Master... I was informed that he had been wounded by a shell and wounded in three places, in the head, arm and breast. He fell from the mare he was riding and we were forced to leave him on the field. I would have gone back if I could, but I could not and even if I had gone, I could not have done any good as his spirit had fled and his soul gone up to Him who gave it. I need not tell you my dear young mistress how I felt. I loved him so much

TRUE GRAY

having been with him so long. I could not for a long time bring myself to believe that he was gone, but at last reality burst forth, and I felt lonesome indeed.

"Richard" to Mrs. Thomas G. Pollock, 1864

We have frequently heard the slaves who accompanied their masters to the "scene of action," assert that when fighting was to be done, they wanted to shoulder their muskets and do their share of it, and we have not a shadow of a doubt but what they would be found perfectly reliable.

Southern Banner, May 1, 1861

Mr. Venable said he did not see a braver thing done than the cool performance of a Columbia negro. He carried his master a bucket of ham and rice, which he had cooked for him, and he cried: "You must be so tired and hungry, marster; make haste and eat." This was in the thickest of the fight, under the heaviest of the enemy's guns.

Mary Boykin Chesnut, on First Manassas, 1861

203

TRUE GRAY

In the recent battle at Belmont, Lieutenant Shelton, of the 18th Arkansas regiment, had his servant Jack in the fight. Both Jack and his master were wounded, but not till they had made the most heroic efforts to drive back the insolent invaders. Finally, after Jack had fired at the enemy twenty-seven times, he fell seriously wounded in the arm.

Daily Sun, November 26, 1861

For a considerable time during the siege the enemy had a Negro rifle shooter in their front who kept up a close fire on our men, and, although the distance was great, yet he caused more or less annoyance by his persistent shooting. On one occasion while at the advance posts with a detail, the writer with his squad had an opportunity to note the skill of this determined darky with his well-aimed rifle.

Capt. C. A. Stevens, Berdan's Sharpshooters, 1862.

This volume is set in Bookman Old Style. Title, chapters, headings and pagination are in Caslon Antique. The book design is by Trickmule Scripts, charcoal portrait of Daniel and Wash by Colin Turner, formatting and typesetting by Emmanuel Flatten, cover graphics by Kristy Watson, Polonyx Graphic Design, LLC.

Made in the USA
Middletown, DE
18 September 2019